CRETE PUB...
1177 N. MAIN
CRETE IL 60417
708/672-8017

WITHDRAWN

P9-DYD-413

Peace and Love Cupcakes

The Cupcake Club

Sheryl Berk and Carrie Berk

sourcebooks
jabberwocky

Copyright © 2012 by Sheryl Berk and Carrie Berk
Cover and internal design © 2012 by Sourcebooks, Inc.
Cover illustration © Julia Denos
Cover design by Rose Audette

Sourcebooks and the colophon are registered trademarks of Sourcebooks, Inc.

All rights reserved. No part of this book may be reproduced in any form
or by any electronic or mechanical means, including information storage
and retrieval systems—except in the case of brief quotations embodied in
critical articles or reviews—without permission in writing from its publisher,
Sourcebooks, Inc.

The characters and events portrayed in this book are fictitious or are used ficti-
tiously. Any similarity to real persons, living or dead, is purely coincidental and
not intended by the author.

Published by Sourcebooks Jabberwocky, an imprint of Sourcebooks, Inc.
P.O. Box 4410, Naperville, Illinois 60567-4410
(630) 961-3900
Fax: (630) 961-2168
www.jabberwockykids.com

Library of Congress Cataloging-in-Publication data is on file with the publisher.

Source of Production: Versa Press, East Peoria, Illinois, USA
Date of Production: February 2012
Run Number: 17727

Printed and bound in the United States of America.
VP 10 9 8 7 6 5 4 3 2 1

To Grandpa "Gee" Eddie Kahn, who taught
us to appreciate the sweet things in life.
We love you always and forever.

A Monstrous Day

Why does it have to be Monday?

Kylie Carson pulled the blanket over her head and pretended not to hear her snooze alarm beeping for the third time. And Monday, November 6, no less! Her fourth-grade teacher, Ms. Shottlan, had asked everyone to pick a topic they were an expert on and share ten fabulous facts about it.

"The idea," her teacher said, "is to wow us!"

The big red circle on the calendar had stared at Kylie for two weeks. By this time, most of the kids had already presented their reports. Emily Dutter talked about horseback riding. Jeremy Saperstone explained about football, and Meredith Mitchell? She went on and on about gymnastics—and held up the three gold medals she won at last year's state championship meet.

But what had *she* chosen to talk about? Monster movies! It was truly the only thing Kylie was an expert on.

Dracula vs. Frankenstein, The Mummy, The Phantom of the Opera. She saw them all a million times! But now that the day was here and the clock said 7:57, she was having second thoughts.

She plopped down in her seat at the kitchen table, still in her peace-sign pj's and fuzzy slippers.

"Is it Pajama Day at school?" her mom teased. "Or are we just starting a new fashion trend?

Kylie groaned. "Expert presentation today."

"Ah-hah!" said her mom. "And you are an expert at being late to school?"

"I don't want to go," said Kylie. "It's going to be a colossal disaster!"

"Colossal disaster, huh? That's a pretty dramatic way to describe a five-minute report in front of your class. But then again, monster movies are very dramatic—so I suppose it's appropriate." Her mom chuckled.

Kylie rolled her eyes. "What if they laugh at me?" she asked. "Or worse…throw things."

"They won't laugh," her mother assured her, tossing another pancake onto Kylie's plate, even though she had barely touched the first one.

"No, trust me, they will. Gavin Gilligan flicked a grape

at Jeremy Saperstone yesterday in the cafeteria—and that was just because Jeremy looked at him funny. One weird look and Jeremy got a grape in his eye! No one in my class likes monster movies. They'll think I'm stupid!"

Her mom handed her the maple syrup. "I think it's a little late to change your mind, don't you? School starts in twenty minutes."

That was it—she was doomed. Doomed like the Wolfman when the sheriff came after him with a gun loaded with silver bullets. The furry fiend knew he was in for an unhappily-ever-after, and Kylie knew the same. She could feel it in her bones. If she could just miss school this one day!

"You know, my throat's a little sore," she said with a cough.

Her mom felt Kylie's head. "Nice try," her mom said. "Cool as a cucumber. Get dressed."

Kylie came out of her room five minutes later, dragging her feet—this time in gray high-top sneakers. She'd chosen her black jeans and a black, long-sleeve tee, because the dark color matched her dark mood.

"Much better," her mom said. Then she handed Kylie her backpack, her lunch box, and the huge poster board she'd made: a collage of the world's greatest monsters at their bloodiest, creepiest, scariest best.

"You'll be great, honey," her mom said, planting a kiss on Kylie's cheek. "It's normal to feel butterflies when you speak in front of a group of people. I always do."

It wasn't so much the group as it was one particular person Kylie was worried about. And it wasn't butterflies she felt in her stomach, it was more like vampire bats. But telling her mom that wouldn't help. Instead she trudged outside and just made the school bus before it pulled away from her corner.

The Sneaker That Started It All

At 9 a.m. sharp, Ms. Shottlan announced, "Time for our expert reports!" Kylie sank down in her chair, hoping somehow, some way her teacher would forget to call on her. Maybe they'd have a fire drill—or a surprise assembly in the auditorium. Maybe Ms. Shottlan would announce it was a national holiday and school would be closed the rest of the day!

Crazier things had happened at Blakely Elementary School. One time a mouse got loose from a classroom, and they'd had to evacuate the entire school for two hours while the teachers looked for the escapee. Kylie closed her eyes tightly and willed some kind of harmless catastrophe to happen so she could get out of class. "Please, please, please, let me *not* have to go today!"

Ms. Shottlan must have read her mind, because she called on Bella Russell first. Kylie breathed a huge sigh of relief.

"I did my report on dogs," Bella said. "Did you know the biggest dog in the world weighed 282 pounds?"

"Wow!" said Jeremy. "That's like four of me!"

Bella went on and on about different breeds of dogs and her adorable cockapoo, Hermione. "She knows how to count to ten barking," Bella bragged.

When Bella had taken her seat, Ms. Shottlan glanced at her plan book. "Let's see," she said, perching her glasses on the tip of her nose. "Whose turn is it next?"

Kylie held her breath. Maybe if she stayed absolutely still as a statue, Ms. Shottlan would pass right over her.

"Kylie! You're up!"

No such luck. "Um, do I have to go *right* now?" Kylie asked. "Can Abby go before me?"

Ms. Shottlan shook her head. "Nope."

Kylie's chair creaked as she pushed it back from her desk. She walked to the front of the room and tried not to look anyone in the eye as she unrolled her poster.

"Eww!" Meredith shouted. "That is so gross!" She covered her eyes. "I can't look!"

Just as Kylie had feared, Meredith was making fun of her presentation—and she hadn't even said a single word yet! Of course, Emily and Bella followed

Meredith's lead. Bella even pretended to swoon and fall off her chair.

Kylie gulped. This wasn't going to be pretty.

"My report is about monster movies," she said quietly. She heard lots of giggles but tried to ignore them.

"Louder, please," said Ms. Shottlan. "So everyone in the back of the room can hear you."

Kylie cleared her throat and continued, "Did you know that vampires can't see their reflection in a mirror? And you can't capture their image in a photo."

"That's not true!" said Gavin. "I saw *Twilight* three times!"

"Yeah," said Meredith. "You're wrong."

"Class!" cried Ms. Shottlan. "Only one student at a time, and it is Kylie's turn to present. Save your comments for the end."

Kylie took a deep breath and continued. "Boris Karloff was an amazing monster-movie actor. He played Frankenstein's monster. And the Mummy and both Jekyll and Hyde." She pointed to each character on her poster.

Meredith yawned. Jeremy pretended to snore. Bella blew a bubble with her gum.

Five minutes felt like five hours! When Kylie finished, Ms. Shottlan applauded and thanked her. "That was a fascinating presentation," she said. "Thank you, Kylie, for teaching us all about monsters."

Meredith whispered to Emily as Kylie walked by, "Of course she'd know all about monsters. She's a *freak*!"

Kylie bit her lip. She wished she had the courage to put Meredith in her place. If she did, she would have shot back, "Oh yeah? Well, you're the Bride of Frankenstein!" Instead Kylie hurried back to her seat and kept quiet. There was simply no use responding. Meredith was so popular and everyone would take her side.

Meredith grinned, then stuck out her tongue. Kylie sighed. She should be used to this by now. It wasn't the first time Meredith Mitchell had called Kylie a name or made fun of her in front of everyone. In fact, Meredith had been doing it for over a year. Kylie didn't know why Meredith always singled her out to embarrass.

But she did know when it had started…back in September of third grade, when Kylie was new to Blakely. That summer, her dad switched jobs and they'd moved from Jupiter, Florida, to New Fairfield, Connecticut. Kylie was excited. She had never seen snow, and her dad promised there would be tons in their new backyard by December. "Enough to go sledding and build a ginormous snowman," he told her.

She was sad to say good-bye to her old friends, Jaimie and Victoria, but she was also excited to live in a big house with a backyard and a new bedroom she could decorate any way she liked. She and her mom had had so much fun poring over catalogs and combing the aisles at Home Depot! Kylie chose a bright lavender paint for the walls (she loved the color name: Brave Purple!), a fuzzy white rug, and a warm down comforter in white with purple peace signs sprinkled all over it.

In the corner of the room, she'd placed a squishy, purple beanbag chair so she could flop on it and read or gaze out the window and daydream. And as a surprise, her mom and dad got her a vintage movie-monster poster—*The Mummy's Curse* with Lon Chaney—and framed and hung it over her desk.

She would miss her apartment in Florida—especially the little wooden playground out back where she used to climb the monkey bars with her friends. But this is pretty awesome, she thought, looking around her new space. Way cooler than the pink, princessy room she'd left behind.

She'd had only a week to anticipate what third grade would be like in Connecticut. Her parents promised it wouldn't be much different from her old school: lots of kids, lots of classes, nice teachers.

"I hear last year they had four snow days," her dad said over breakfast.

"What's a snow day?" Kylie asked, her mouth filled with Cocoa Puffs.

"It's a free day to sleep late, go sledding, goof off," her dad explained. "If the roads get too snowy, they can't get the school buses through. So you get to stay home."

Kylie's eyes widened. "Really? No school when it snows? That's amazing!"

"Let's hope there aren't too many snow days this year," her mom teased.

The first day of third grade wasn't bad at all. The kids seemed friendly, and her teacher, Ms. Levenhart, let them decorate frames with their photos to hang on the classroom door. The first week flew by, and Kylie couldn't believe how much homework she had already—reading, writing, math, and spelling every night!

"Did you make any friends?" her mom asked, over a plate of milk and cookies after school near the end of that week. While she munched her snack at the kitchen counter, Kylie was already tackling her math worksheet, focused on a hard word problem about Ms. Levenhart having 125 pencils and needing to divide them evenly among the class.

"Well, these kids have all known each other since kindergarten," Kylie explained. "But this one girl, Emily, showed me a mistake I made in multiplication."

Her mom perched her glasses on the tip of her nose so she could look over the top of them. Kylie knew what that meant: her mom was worried about something and about to lecture her.

"Honey, your dad and I think it would be a good idea if you signed up for some after-school clubs, got involved…"

Kylie was too busy calculating: how many times did 18 go into 125? Was it 6 or 7? She counted on her fingers.

"Kylie? Did you hear what I said?" Her mom sighed.

"Yeah, after-school club. Got it!" she replied. But she meant she got the solution to the math problem—not what her mom was asking her to do.

"What about chess club? Or the tennis one? I loved tennis when I was your age."

Kylie wrinkled her nose. "Seriously? I don't know how to play chess. And I'm terrible at tennis. Remember the time I served the ball to Dad and almost broke his nose?"

Her mom nodded. "Oh yeah. Forgot about that. Well,

there must be something fun you can do after school." She picked up the flyer Kylie had brought home listing all the Blakely Elementary extracurriculars.

"Hip-hop club! That sounds fun…I mean, way awesome!" her mom enthused. Kylie giggled. It was pretty funny when her mother tried to sound "cool." She'd toss in words like "awesome" or "all that" or "LOL." The day before, when Kylie had told her mom she was right about it being chilly and Kylie needing a jacket, her mom replied, "TYS!"—and then had to explain that was short for "Told you so!"

Kylie thought a minute. How bad could the hip-hop club be? Hip-hop dancing looked so easy in music videos. You just kind of jumped around to the music. You didn't have to be a particularly graceful dancer—a good thing, in her case!

"Okay, okay," she sighed. "I'll try it."

Her mom smiled and kissed Kylie on the top of her head. "That's my girl!"

Kylie showed up the next day for auditions in the auditorium. About a dozen kids were trying out.

But Meredith Mitchell was the one who had everyone's attention. She was break-dancing, pop-n-locking, and turning perfect cartwheels on the stage. All the kids were in awe.

And so was Kylie. Meredith was practically perfect—and everything Kylie wasn't. She had bright blue eyes and long, shiny blond hair that fell in soft ringlets around her shoulders. Kylie thought her own hair was the color of mud, and she had her dad's hazel eyes—sometimes brown, sometimes green. It was as if they couldn't make up their mind!

Meredith wore a trendy tie-dyed hoodie with a big peace sign studded on the back, designer jeans, and a sparkly barrette that matched her outfit. Kylie was in her cousin Zoe's hand-me-down jeans and a boring gray tee. And then there was Meredith's bling—a beautiful, sparkly diamond M charm around her neck that glittered under the spotlight on stage.

"Kylie Carson?" Ms. Sattin, the dance club adviser, called. It took three times before Kylie heard her name. How would she ever be as amazing as Meredith? She walked to the center of the stage.

"Show us what you've got, Kylie!" said Ms. Sattin.

The music started and Kylie tried to find her groove to "Evacuate the Dance Floor." Out of the corner of her eye, she could see Meredith in the front row of the auditorium, laughing and pointing. I'll show her, Kylie thought. She made up her own wild moves—a combination of break dancing, the Electric Slide, and the Dougie. She knew her steps were no way as flawless as Meredith's, but she hoped her grand finale would wow everyone.

She decided to perform a chorus-line kick, like she had seen the Rockettes do during Macy's Thanksgiving Day Parade on TV. She pumped her leg higher and higher until it was over her head. Then—like slow motion in a movie—Kylie kicked so hard that her pink Converse sneaker went flying through the air. It landed with a thud in Meredith's face.

"My eye!" screamed Meredith. All the kids and Ms. Sattin raced over. Meredith's eye was red and already swelling.

Oh no! It was just like the time she'd served the tennis ball right at her dad's unsuspecting nose. "I'm so sorry!" Kylie pleaded.

And as they were taking Meredith away to the school nurse, she growled, "I will *destroy* you, Kylie Carson!" Kylie didn't *think* Meredith meant it. She was just hurt and upset, and she had an ugly black eye for a week. Of course, Kylie didn't make the squad. But ever since that day, Meredith had made it her mission to make Kylie miserable. The mean whispers and nasty names ("Creature! Blob! Ghoul!") were one thing, but lately Meredith had gone even further.

Last week, while Kylie was getting off the school bus with her social studies diorama, a model of a Japanese tea ceremony, Kylie had accidentally tripped down the bus steps and landed in a huge mud puddle on Frisbee Street. The bus driver rushed to help her up.

"You okay? You gotta watch where you're stepping there, young lady," he said.

When Kylie wiped the mud out of her eyes, she saw Meredith in the front seat, grinning like an evil, mad scientist. Meredith glanced down at her foot and tapped it. Kylie fumed. Her diorama was crushed—and so was her pride.

She thought about telling someone—her parents, her teacher—but she suspected that would only make Meredith madder. So she just took the abuse. Even when Meredith snapped a picture of Kylie sneezing applesauce out of her nose in the cafeteria and showed it to everyone on her cell phone. Kylie ignored it, hoping one day Meredith would get bored with bullying her.

Unfortunately, today was not that day.

Florida hadn't been like this. Kylie had tons of friends

there who loved to go shopping and to the movies and to have sleepovers. But being the new girl instantly made her an outsider—an alien invader. Coming from a city named Jupiter didn't help. When Meredith found that out, she started calling Kylie "E.T."

Making friends had been hard before, but now it was impossible. Meredith made sure of that. Anytime Emily, Bella, or Abby tried to talk to Kylie, Meredith quickly stepped in and yanked them away. "Let's go!" she'd command, and they followed her like puppies on a leash. A few of the girls spoke to Kylie in the school yard, but she always felt like "the new girl" and a loner, even after a whole year at Blakely. The only time Kylie felt like she truly fit in was in Ms. Rachel Valentine's drama class. She just wished they had it more than twice a week.

Kylie loved Ms. Valentine. She was funny, and she always smelled like vanilla. Plus, she love, love, loved old Hollywood movies—stuff like *Gone with the Wind* and *Top Hat* and all those silly Mickey Rooney–Judy Garland flicks. "Now those were the days!" she'd sigh, and click her heels together while doing a little leap in the air.

Kylie would crack up. Ms. Valentine looked silly tap-dancing in her Ugg boots. But that was the thing about Ms. Valentine: she just didn't care what people thought. She did what made her happy, what made her feel good. Kylie wished she could be that "footloose and fancy free," as her teacher liked to call it. Instead she felt weighed down by a huge, heavy anchor. Its name was Meredith Mitchell.

But today Ms. Valentine had come to class looking a little more serious than usual. "Class," she began, "I have something I need to talk to you about. You see, I have some good news—some great news!"

If her news is so great, Kylie thought, then why does she look so nervous?

"You see," she said, drumming her fingers on the desk, "My husband and I have been trying to have a baby for a long, long time. And, well, I'm having a baby—actually two of them. Twins!"

Most of the girls in class erupted into "oohs" and "ahhs," while the boys made faces. Kylie just sat there, frozen.

"I'm due in the summer, but my husband got a great job in Los Angeles working as a production assistant on a TV series. So we're going to move there before the babies come."

Kylie didn't hear much of anything after the word "move." It was as if Ms. Valentine was speaking a different language. Did she say she was leaving? Did she say she was not going to be their teacher anymore?

"I am going to ask your new drama teacher to start next week so she can get to know all of you and so I can help make the transition a little easier."

Next week? Kylie didn't want a new drama teacher next week. She didn't want a new drama teacher *ever*. She didn't want anyone but Ms. Valentine! Without her, there would be absolutely, positively *nothing* to look forward to about fourth grade.

After drama class was over, Ms. Valentine stopped Kylie before she left the room.

"I know you're going to like the new teacher—and she'll like you," Ms. Valentine said. "And we'll stay in touch, I promise."

Kylie nodded, but she knew emails and letters wouldn't be the same—she practically never spoke anymore to her friends in Florida. Ms. Valentine was the only one who made Kylie feel smart and, well, normal.

"I have something for you," Ms. Valentine said, pulling a DVD from her tote bag. "*Annie Get Your Gun* was my favorite musical when I was your age." Kylie looked at the cover. It had a weird freckled cowgirl on it.

"Annie isn't like other girls—she kind of marches to her own drummer. But in the end, she's a star," Ms. Valentine explained. Then she sang: "There's no business like show business, like no business I know…"

"Uh-huh" was all Kylie could say. A dumb DVD couldn't make up for the fact that Ms. Valentine was abandoning her. Nothing could.

The new drama teacher wrote her name in bright red script on the Smart Board: Ms. Juliette Dubois. Her signature had so many loops and swirls that it looked like an autograph. But Ms. Dubois didn't *look* like a movie star. In fact, she looked more like a kid than a teacher. She wore jeans and a pink Abercrombie tee, and her hair was in a long strawberry-blond ponytail down her back.

"Ms. *Duh-boys*?" Jeremy tried to pronounce it.

"It's *Doo-bwah*," Meredith corrected him. "It's French. My mother took me to Paris last summer, so I know how to speak French fluently."

Ms. Dubois raised an eyebrow at Meredith. "*Oui?*" Then she began chatting away at her in French.

Meredith swallowed hard. "Um, *bonjour*?"

Kylie tried not to laugh. Maybe this teacher wouldn't be so bad…not if she could make Meredith squirm!

"Well, luckily I will be teaching this class in English," Ms. Dubois continued. "Although I am from Quebec and we speak a lot of French there. You can all call me Juliette."

Juliette told them all about playing Juliet in the Stratford Shakespeare Festival's production of *Romeo and Juliet*. The kids were all impressed—especially when she demonstrated how she got to die dramatically in the play. She pretended to plunge a dagger into her heart and collapsed in a twitching heap on the floor.

"We're going to have a lot of fun in this class," she insisted. "Starting with our first performance in two weeks. We're going to stage a play for the school's Wellness Day."

Then she handed out small index cards with different foods drawn on them. Bella got a carrot, Jeremy got a box of cereal, and Meredith got a bottle of milk.

"Cool!" said Abby. "I'm a watermelon. I can spit seeds at the audience!"

Kylie looked at her card. There was a funny-looking white circle with green lines sticking out of it. "What is this?" she asked.

"Oh! That's a turnip," smiled Juliette. "Whatever food is on your card will be your role in the play."

Kylie groaned. Why couldn't she at least be something

people would recognize, like a crunchy apple or a funny banana? "Turnips don't do anything," she complained. "They just sit there!"

"Then it's the perfect role for you," Meredith muttered.

"Every food is fun—I promise," Juliette said.

Kylie couldn't imagine what could be fun about being a turnip. And it only got worse when they started rehearsals a few days later. Jack Yu, who had been cast as the farmer, was trying to yank her out of the soil.

"Dig deep!" Juliette told him. "Pull, pull, pull! And, Kylie, you act like a really stubborn root."

Easier said than done. Jack was nearly twice her size, and he was yanking her arm out of the socket.

"Now rise, rise, rise, turnip—and squint, like you're seeing the sun for the very first time," Juliette instructed.

Kylie tried to rise gracefully, but the moment she got to her feet, Jack suddenly let go—and she fell back to the stage with a hard *thud*.

"Ow!" Kylie said, rubbing her bruised butt. "You're not supposed to drop me!"

Jack shrugged. "I have other vegetables to pick."

☆ ☮ ☆

That night Kylie had a horrible nightmare. Meredith was shoveling dirt on top of her as the audience roared with laughter. Even Ms. Valentine was there in the front row, bouncing her two babies on her lap and cheering. The dirt kept piling up, burying Kylie alive under a mountain of mulch. She gasped for air and tried to scream for help, but she couldn't get the words out.

"Honey, you okay?" her mom asked, shaking Kylie gently. "You were having a bad dream. It sounded like you were screaming, 'I'm not a vegetable!'"

Kylie woke in a cold sweat—and swore she could taste dirt in the back of her throat. "Yeah, I'm okay," she lied, and let her mom tuck her back under the covers and rub her back. "Just a stupid dream about being a turnip."

"I didn't know turnips were so terrifying," her mom said, kissing Kylie's forehead. "This from the girl who didn't bat an eyelash watching *Zombie Prom*?"

Kylie closed her eyes. She didn't want to talk about it. Sometimes real life in elementary school was a lot scarier than horror movies.

She didn't feel any better the next morning when she saw everyone's costumes for the first time at dress rehearsal. Jack looked like a real farmer in a pair of mud-stained overalls, a plaid shirt, and a cowboy hat. He was chewing on a drinking straw. "I couldn't find a piece of real straw," he explained.

Abby the Watermelon had a red-and-black polka-dot leotard and a green ruffled skirt. Juliette wouldn't let Abby spit at the audience, but she was allowed to throw black confetti at them as she said her line, "Careful not to swallow my seeds!"

Meredith's mother had had a costume custom-made for her so she could play a bottle of milk in all its glory. "This is 100 percent silk," Meredith told Bella. "And chiffon—feel!" Then she said her line: "Milk builds strong teeth and bones, strengthens your immune system, and makes your skin glow." She twirled around in a circle so that the layers of her costume swirled around her in a delicate cloud.

Kylie looked down at her costume: a pair of white bike shorts and a white tank top. On her head, she had tied a Styrofoam paper plate with green pipe cleaners poked through it. She thought it looked pretty authentic, and Juliette had said it was very creative. But compared to Meredith—who looked more like an angel than a glass of milk—Kylie was a disaster.

Meredith apparently agreed. "She looks like something you'd throw up," she hissed behind Kylie's back. Abby and Bella giggled.

That was it! Kylie couldn't take it anymore! Her dad had always told her it was important to stand up for herself, hadn't he? She was so mad that she didn't even worry what everyone thought. She spun around, her hands clenched in fists at her sides. "You know what you are, Meredith?" she began.

Meredith batted her eyelashes and smiled. The rest of the class gathered around them, sensing a fight. Kylie was surrounded by all the brightly colored fruits and veggies. She felt like she was standing in the middle of a giant salad bowl.

"What?" Meredith taunted her.

Kylie blurted out, "You're…you're…*sour milk*!"

Meredith laughed. "Really? That's the best you can do?" She came closer, almost nose to nose with Kylie, staring right into her eyes. Kylie didn't blink—not once.

"What's going on here?" Juliette asked, carrying a cardboard tree from backstage.

"Nothing," smiled Meredith, backing off. "Just practicing my lines!"

"Everything okay, Kylie?" Juliette asked.

Kylie nodded. "Fine."

But of course it wasn't. She could feel the stares and hear the laughter of her classmates. The only thing she had done by standing up for herself was make things worse.

Friday at final rehearsal, Meredith was at it again. "You know my mother sent my portfolio to a modeling agency in New York," she bragged to Bella. "The agent thinks I'd be perfect for *Teen Vogue.*"

Then she turned to Kylie. "You know, you should model," she said. Kylie raised an eyebrow. She knew there was more coming. Meredith would *never* pay her a compliment.

"Huh?" Bella asked. "Her?"

"Sure," Meredith said with a smirk. "Kylie could be the cover of next month's *American Ghoul!*" She and Bella rolled on the stage laughing.

Kylie winced at the stupid joke. This time she wasn't taking the bait. She remembered how her mom always reminded her, "Sticks and stones may break my bones, but names will never hurt me." Nice in concept, but tougher in real life. Sometimes words were just as bad as a bee sting. They pricked.

"I didn't realize dress rehearsals were so hilarious,"

27

Juliette interrupted. Meredith sat up and covered her mouth, trying to hide her giggles.

"Once again from the top," Juliette said, summoning them back to their places on stage.

Kylie stood in the back row of "the garden" while Meredith fluttered around the stage. "I could do an arabesque at the end," she suggested.

"I don't think a glass of milk would really do an arabesque," Juliette said. "But if you're feeling it…"

"Oh, I am!" Meredith said, making another graceful twirl. "I am totally feeling it!"

Kylie rolled her eyes. Meredith was trying to steal the spotlight—and she was doing a pretty good job of it. Why didn't Juliette notice? Why didn't anyone else care that she was turning Wellness Day into Meredith Day? They were all mesmerized by her graceful twirls and pliés—just as everyone had been at the hip-hop club auditions. That was the thing about Meredith: she knew how to suck people in. Kylie didn't know how she did it. If Kylie still believed in fairy tales, she'd swear Meredith had cast an evil spell that made everyone in Blakely worship her. And if there was ever anyone with Wicked Witch potential…

"Okay, great. Thanks, Meredith!" Juliette said. Thank

goodness her teacher had come to her senses! "Maybe you could do a lovely little curtsey at the end?"

Meredith beamed and took a bow, stepping hard on Kylie's foot in the process.

"Ow!" Kylie yelped.

"Oh, my bad!" Meredith said.

When Juliette was out of earshot she added, "Maybe you should stand a little farther back…like maybe Jupiter?"

"What is your problem?" Kylie asked as the bell rang for the next period.

"I don't have a problem." Meredith grinned innocently. Then she linked arms with Emily and Bella and strolled out of the auditorium. "I just can't *wait* for the play," she said, glancing back at Kylie.

4

The Show Must Go On

When the day of the play finally arrived, Kylie's stomach was in knots. The auditorium was packed with students, teachers, and parents. "Places, everybody!" Juliette called backstage. "Remember to enunciate and project!"

All the grades had gathered in the auditorium for the performance of *Food on Parade!* Kylie's part came at the very end of the show, right before the procession of healthy foods.

"Turnips provide an excellent source of vitamin C and fiber," she said. As Jack pulled her from the pile of dirt (really a bunch of brown construction paper), she jumped to her feet. "You can also eat my leaves. They're called turnip greens." Then she tried to remove a green pipe cleaner from her hat. Funny, but it wouldn't come loose. So she tried another, then another. They wouldn't budge.

"Leave the greens—it's okay," Juliette whispered from the wings. But Kylie was determined.

"What's wrong with this?" She huffed and puffed, trying not to tear her entire hat apart.

The kids in the audience started to giggle, and Kylie felt her cheeks flush bright red.

"Look," called a fifth grader from the audience. "She's a *red* turnip now!" Everyone cracked up—even a few of the teachers.

Kylie felt like running off the stage, but she stuck it out, marching with the rest of her class in the parade of healthy foods. After they had taken their bows, she untied the plate from her head and checked the pipe cleaners. They had been hot-glued into her hat. She didn't even need to ask who had done it.

"Wardrobe malfunction?" Juliette found her backstage. "It happens to the best of them."

Kylie wondered if she should rat Meredith out to their teacher. That would feel *so* good, but she didn't actually have proof and didn't want to sound whiny. So she answered, "Yeah, I guess I got a little carried away with the Krazy Glue."

"I see," said Juliette. "Kylie, could I have a word?"

Kylie's heart started to pound. Was she in trouble for ruining the play? Would Juliette blame her and send her to the principal? This was awful! And worse, it wasn't her fault.

Juliette patted a bench backstage. "Have a seat."

Kylie sat next to her, staring down at her sneakers and dreading what was coming.

"I think someone played a nasty prank on you," Juliette said. "Am I right?"

Kylie heaved a huge sigh of relief. "Yes!" she said.

"Do you know who?"

She shook her head and lied, "No. Not really."

"Well, you know, when I was your age, I was picked on all the time. I had these horrible thick glasses and freckles, and hair that was practically neon red! I used to think it was the color of red velvet cupcakes."

Kylie twirled a strand of her own hair around her finger. "Wow," she said. "That must have been really hard."

"It was, but it made me the person I am today." Juliette reached into her purse and pulled out a small plastic container. In it was a red velvet cupcake, iced with a mountain of white cream-cheese frosting and dusted with crunchy brown-sugar crystals.

"Have a taste," Juliette said. "I baked it myself from scratch. My grandma Gaga's recipe. Now red velvet is my favorite."

33

Kylie took a lick of the frosting, and it melted in her mouth. It had a hint of maple flavor that reminded her of her mom's pancakes. Then she bit into the moist red cake; it was rich, chocolaty heaven.

"This is amazing!" Kylie said.

"Glad you think so. Because I have an idea, and I think you're just the person to pull it off."

Kylie licked the last bits of frosting from her fingertips. She'd practically inhaled the scrumptious cupcake. "Me?"

"You see, when I was being picked on, Gaga taught me how to bake. I would bring in delicious cakes and treats for my class. And guess what?"

"What?" asked Kylie.

"Pretty soon, everyone—even the mean kids who picked on me—were *begging* me to bake more for them."

Kylie mulled it over. "So what you're saying is, if I bake cupcakes, kids will like me?" It was a little hard to believe.

"I'm saying give it a try. I was thinking of starting a baking club after school. Will you help me? Recruit some kids for the first meeting next Wednesday? And you can be the first member—the president!"

Kylie liked the sound of that. "Um, okay," she said. "I guess I could make some flyers and put them up."

"Fabulous!" said Juliette. "I bet our club will be the most popular club in school in no time."

5

Cooking Up a Club

Early Monday morning, Kylie woke up in a great mood. She danced around her bedroom, rocking out to the radio. The dream she'd had the night before about the baking club was amazing. She was wearing a white puffy chef's hat and presenting a giant baby-shower cake shaped like a baby bottle to Ms. Valentine.

"Oh, Kylie! You shouldn't have!" Ms. Valentine gushed in the dream. *"This is the most beautiful cake I have ever seen!"*

Everyone in the auditorium applauded and gave Kylie a standing ovation. She bowed and waved to her adoring fans. Wouldn't that be nice? she thought as she skipped out of her room.

"What's the rush today, Smiley Kylie?" her dad, Peter, teased. "You even beat me to the Cheerios box!"

Kylie gobbled up her breakfast, leaving just a few O's swimming in her bowl. "Can you drive me to school today on your way to work, Dad?" she asked. "I want to get there super early. I have some posters to hang up."

"Sure," her father replied, checking his watch as he grabbed a banana from the fruit bowl. "But this ship sets sail in three minutes. Are you on board, matey?"

Kylie saluted. "Aye-aye, Captain Pete!" she giggled. Sometimes her dad treated her like a little girl instead of a fourth grader, calling her Smiley Kylie and still assuming she liked to play pirates like they did when she was five. But he made her laugh—especially when he limped out the front door, pretending to have a peg leg. She felt so happy and energized this morning that nothing—not even her dad singing, "Yo-ho-ho and a bottle of Snapple!" in the car on the way to school—could bother her.

After her dad dropped her at the school steps, she raced inside to post a bright yellow sign on the cafeteria bulletin board: "Baking Club Meets This Wednesday! Sign Up Now!" She'd made the poster herself, dotting each "I" with a sparkly cupcake sticker and including twenty lines for kids to write their names. The students were just beginning to file in, and Emily from her class peered over her shoulder.

"Do you want to join?" Kylie asked her hopefully.

"Well…" Emily began.

But Meredith jumped in. "What's a *baking* club?" she said with a sniff. "I'm on the gymnastics team, in the hip-hop club, on the student council…" She turned to Emily. "Who has time for a lame baking club?"

"Yeah," Emily reconsidered. "I'm pretty busy. Ballet three times a week."

"Oh," said Kylie. "Okay." She couldn't mask her disappointment. Emily had looked genuinely interested until Meredith butted in.

When Kylie checked back at recess, no one had signed up yet. At the end of the day, there was only one name on the poster: "Ivanna Throwup." As Kylie was crossing out the nasty joke, a little girl walked up and stared at the poster.

"What's your name?" asked Kylie.

"Brynn," the girl said, shuffling her feet.

"Do you want to join?" Kylie practically begged.

"Um, I'm in kindergarten," the girl replied.

"That's okay!" said Kylie. "K-5 is welcome!"

"I can't read. I don't know what the sign says. I just liked the cupcake stickers."

Kylie sighed, peeling off a chocolate one. "Here ya go," she said. Brynn beamed and skipped off.

Kylie found Juliette in the drama classroom. "This is *not* working," she complained, handing the stack of flyers to her teacher. "Nobody wants to join. Maybe baking was popular in Quebec, but it's not in Connecticut. We should just forget the whole thing."

"Hmm, very surprising," Juliette replied.

"That no one would join?" Kylie asked.

"No," said her teacher, "that you're a quitter. I never thought you would be."

"I am not a quitter!" Kylie protested. "It's just…"

"It's just that sometimes things don't happen right away. Stick with it, and you'll find kids who want to belong to a great club."

"But everyone says they're too busy," Kylie explained.

"Maybe *some* kids are too busy." Juliette handed Kylie back the flyers. "But some kids aren't. All you need are four members, and Principal Fontina will let us use the kitchen in the teachers' lounge to meet."

"Okay, I'll try again."

"Good!" said Juliette. "I knew I wasn't wrong about you."

From then on, Kylie decided to take matters into her own hands. No more flyers or posters—she was going to personally ask all her classmates, one by one if she had to, and find members for the Blakely baking club. Together, they'd bake the most amazingly delicious treats, just like she had dreamed the night before. And not even Meredith could take that away from her.

Jenna-normous

Jenna Medina was sitting alone on a bench in the school yard while the fourth graders hung out at recess. She was heavier than most of the girls at Blakely—and she got teased about it all the time. Kylie had overheard girls in the bathroom making fun of Jenna. They called her Thunder Thighs, Bubble Butt, even Jenna-normous.

Kylie was very impressed that Jenna ignored the name-calling, held her head high, and walked right past the girls as if they weren't there. She didn't get angry or burst into tears, and she didn't apologize for looking different. She was a bigger person, and she was going to *act* like the bigger person, no matter how mean the kids acted toward her.

Beyond appearances, Kylie didn't know much about Jenna, except that she came from a family of five kids who lived in a small house on the edge of town. She'd heard her mom mention that after she came home from a PTA meeting: "That Mrs. Medina seems like a nice person, but she has an awful lot on her plate. Five kids to raise alone!"

When Kylie asked where Jenna's father was, her mom had shrugged. "She didn't really say—but I hear he just took off and left one day. It's really sad." Her mom also told Kylie that Jenna had two older sisters and twin younger brothers—which put her smack in the middle.

Kylie suspected the Medinas didn't have a lot of money: Jenna's clothes always looked worn out and a little baggy on her—probably hand-me-downs from her big sisters, who were already in middle school. Nonetheless, Jenna seemed okay with it.

When Kylie approached Jenna in the yard, she was eating a six-pack of Oreo cookies. She had cookie crumbs all over her jacket and in the corners of her mouth. It was a good thing she wore her long brown hair in a braid, thought Kylie, or she would've had a cookie-crumb 'do too!

"Hi, I'm Kylie," she said. "Can I sit down?"

Jenna inched over on the bench, making a spot for her.

"Um, you like cookies?" Kylie began.

Jenna looked puzzled. "Are you making fun of me?" she asked.

"No! I would never do that to anyone. I hate when people make fun of me," Kylie protested.

Jenna nodded. "Oh yeah—they call you Freak, right?" she said. "That's probably worse than Fatty."

Kylie's cheeks flushed. Had Meredith gotten to everyone in the school? She was humiliated, which is why Jenna quickly added, "Maybe you should buy Meredith Mitchell a dictionary or something—so she can come up with some new names to call you. Freak's getting pretty old, don't you think?"

She paused…and smiled mischievously. "Oh, wait! That won't work. Meredith has to be able to *read* to use a dictionary!"

Kylie laughed. So Jenna didn't think she was a freak after all. In fact, she was taking Kylie's side and trying to make her feel better.

"Thanks," she said. "Not a lot of kids would be brave enough to say anything against Meredith."

"She doesn't scare me," Jenna said. "If she gets too mean…well, I'll just smush her like a bug." She stamped her feet for emphasis, and the entire bench shook. Kylie inched a little farther away, but then Jenna smiled and handed her a cookie. "Relax! I don't really mean it!"

Jenna was tough on the outside, that's for sure. But Kylie suspected that deep down inside she was really a softie. Kind of like an Oreo cookie sandwich with a sweet, creamy filling.

"How do you do it?" Kylie asked.

"Do what?"

"Just not let them get to you. I try, believe me. But sometimes—"

"You want to just tell the world to leave you alone and…bug off?" Jenna swatted at a fly trying to get near her Oreos.

"Exactly! But if I do, Meredith always twists it. She's much better at this mean-girl thing than I am."

"My advice: don't sink to her level," Jenna replied. "That's what my big sister Gabby always tells me. That's how bullies work—they want you to see you crumble. Meredith just wants to make you mad or scared, and when you are…well, you embarrass yourself in front of everyone. Why let her win?"

"Because she *does* make me mad and scared. I'm really bad at hiding it."

"Hmmm. Okay, call me something really mean," Jenna volunteered.

"Huh? You want me to make fun of you?"

"Yup. Take your best shot. And make it original—I am all about originality. Jack actually called me *grande* in Spanish class yesterday, and I was really impressed. You get extra points if you insult me in another language."

Kylie bit her lip. She didn't want to hurt Jenna's feelings.

"I mean it. Let me have it: Fatso, Chubby-Wubby, Big Stuff…"

Kylie winced. "Oh no! I just can't."

"I won't be upset, I promise. This is practice for how to deal with Meredith. Go!" Jenna elbowed her in the ribs.

Kylie closed her eyes and tried to think of something mean to call Jenna. "Cream puff!" she shouted.

Jenna cracked up. "*Cream puff?* Seriously? Is that supposed to be insulting? I love cream puffs!"

"I'm sorry," Kylie apologized. "I have baking club on the brain. It was the only thing I could think of!"

"Okay, I'll pretend it's mean. Try again."

Kylie repeated, "Cream puff!" and watched Jenna's expression change. Her mouth transformed from a smile into a hard, straight line. Her face became cold, stony, and unbreakable. Kylie gulped. It was pretty scary!

"You see? That's how you do it. The next time Meredith

tosses one at you, you give her that face. She won't know what hit her—and I guarantee it will shut her up. At least long enough for you to walk away."

Kylie nodded. "Thanks. I can't do that face as well as you, but I'll try." Then she remembered why she had approached Jenna in the first place. "Do you want to join my baking club?" Kylie asked.

Jenna took another bite of cookie. "Maybe," she replied. "I do like my mom's baking. She makes the most awesome *dulce de leche* cake!"

Kylie handed her a flyer. "I promise you won't be sorry!" she practically begged. "It will be *really* fun."

"Hey, if we make devil's food cake, we can ask Meredith to join us," Jenna joked. "Get it? *Devil's* food?"

Kylie laughed. "I get it. You crack me up, Jenna."

"I try," she replied. "And I'll try to make it to your baking club meeting tomorrow."

Score! Kylie felt like jumping up and down, but she kept her excitement to herself in case anyone was watching. She had her very first member! With just one day to go before the first meeting, she needed to recruit two more.

The Invisible Girl

In art class the next period, the baking club was all Kylie could think about—which is why when Ms. Bayder asked the class to do a still life, Kylie painted a giant chocolate-chip cookie.

"That's, uh, *interesting*, Kylie," Ms. Bayder said, eyeing her work. It looked like a big yellow blob with brown polka dots.

Then her teacher walked to the easel behind Kylie's and gasped. "Lexi! What an amazing work of art!"

Kylie looked up from the brown dots on her canvas to see Ms. Bayder holding up a flawless painting of blue hydrangeas in a vase. They looked so real that Kylie could almost smell the flowers in bloom. Then Kylie focused on Lexi Poole and realized she was mortified. Lexi looked as white as a ghost. When Ms. Bayder finally put Lexi's painting down, the panic left the girl's face and she went back to work.

Poor Lexi. She was shy and just hated to be the center of attention. Kylie had seen her panic so many times in art class or when Ms. Shottlan called on her. In early October Ms. Shottlan had asked Lexi to give a book report in front of the class. All Lexi could do was sputter out the title of the book, *The Lightning Thief*, before she turned green, clutched her stomach, and hurled. It was pretty gross, but Kylie still felt sorry for her. Lexi had spent the rest of the day in the nurse's office recovering.

For her expert presentation, Lexi had passed out twenty copies of a report—complete with color photos—she had written on Impressionist art. Ms. Shottlan scratched her head. "This is very uh, *impressive*, Lexi, but can you please stand in front of the class and share with us?"

Lexi had thought of that—and she had a plan that required minimal speaking, minimal embarrassment. She rested a large canvas on the Smart Board ledge. A hush fell over the room. It was a breathtaking watercolor of a lake filled with water lilies peeking out from behind a curtain of weeping willow trees. It kind of reminded Kylie of Lexi—like the water lilies, she liked to stay hidden away.

Lexi cleared her throat and said quietly, "My favorite

paintings are Claude Monet's water lilies. This is how I would paint them." Then she took her seat.

Ms. Shottlan nodded. "That was short, sweet, and to the point, but your art speaks for itself. Just gorgeous, Lexi. Why doesn't everyone take a few moments to read her report and then we'll discuss it."

Lexi's cheeks flushed—especially when she caught Kylie staring at her. Kylie looked away. She didn't want Lexi to have another throw-up incident on her account. Instead she looked at the painting. It was truly beautiful—especially the rays of sunlight dancing on the lake's surface. Lexi was super-talented. If I could paint like that, Kylie thought, I'd tell everyone. I'd paint a billboard!

But she understood a little why Lexi chose not to brag. Most geniuses are loners—like Dr. Frankenstein when he was building his monster or Dr. Jekyll when he was perfecting his potion. Brilliance never likes company. Then again, all those people were also pretty crazy. She hoped Lexi wasn't a horror movie fan too. Kylie wouldn't want her to get any ideas!

"Meredith? Do you have a comment about Lexi's report?" Ms. Shottlan asked suddenly.

"Um, sure. It's great." Meredith smiled sweetly. "I bet her portraits are even more beautiful."

Kylie had always wondered why Meredith didn't pick on Lexi too. Then she spotted the picture taped inside Meredith's loose-leaf binder. Meredith had asked (well, actually commanded) Lexi to draw her in a pink, flowing evening gown on a red carpet accepting an Academy Award. When Lexi handed Meredith a portrait in colored pencils, she loved it—so she was leaving Lexi alone for the time being. Lexi might not have had any enemies, but her shyness made it impossible for her to make friends.

As if that wasn't bad enough, her big sister was legendary at Blakely. Ava Poole had been captain of the math team and had an entire shelf of trophies dedicated to her in the library. At graduation the year before, Ava, of course, was chosen to give the "Moving Up" speech in front of the entire school in the auditorium. She explained how school was like a math equation: all the years at Blakely added up to the perfect sum of what you need to go to middle school.

Her speech was pretty clever, Kylie recalled, but it could have used a little more excitement. Maybe a few sound effects? She'd looked around and noticed that some of the kids were falling asleep in their seats.

But the teachers had loved it—they gave Ava a standing ovation. Principal Fontina gushed, "What will we do without you?"

Then Kylie had caught a glimpse of Lexi in one of the last rows. She didn't look proud or happy for her sister. She looked nervous—as if her sibling's speech might somehow cast a spotlight on her.

At the end of presentation of diplomas, everyone had rushed the stage to congratulate the graduates. Kylie didn't know many of the fifth graders and had to go to the bathroom badly. That was where she recognized a pair of Keds sneakers, elaborately colored with markers, poking out from under a stall door. It was positively Lexi. Kylie thought about saying something—then reconsidered. If Lexi had wanted someone to talk to, she wouldn't have hidden in the bathroom.

Now they were in fourth grade—and Ava was in middle school, probably computing Einstein-like equations there as well. If I were Lexi, Kylie thought, I'd be happy to be out of Ava's shadow this year. But Lexi didn't seem too thrilled. Ava was a really hard act to follow, and now everyone at Blakely was looking to Lexi to take her sister's place. That was the last thing Lexi wanted. She preferred to remain invisible—even when she was really good at something.

Lexi had gotten a perfect 100 percent on every spelling test. Yet when Principal Fontina told Lexi she had qualified to compete in the statewide spelling bee, she almost fainted. The very idea of standing in front of an audience and spelling words *out loud*...on TV, no less! She asked her mom to explain that her new braces were too tight and hurt too much for her to speak. No matter how much her parents and sister pleaded with her, Lexi refused to compete.

Kylie felt bad for her, but Lexi's shyness and art talent had given her a great idea.

"Hey, Lexi," she whispered, leaning over the top of her classmate's easel. "Can I talk to you a sec?"

Lexi didn't look up. She just kept working intensely on her hydrangea painting. She didn't even seem to notice that the ends of her long blond hair were dipped in the cup of sky-blue paint.

"Lexi?" Kylie was persistent. "I have this baking club, and we could really use your artistic skills with our cake decorating."

Lexi didn't answer.

"Did you hear me?" Kylie spoke a little louder. "A baking club on Wednesdays after school."

Still no reply. So Kylie threw in, "We only have two members, me and Jenna Medina. So you don't have to worry about a big crowd or anything."

Nada. Kylie took another piece of paper and drew a chocolate cake—or at least her attempt at a chocolate cake—with the word "PLEASE" on top in big, red bubble letters. She placed it on Lexi's easel.

"I know I'm a really bad artist," Kylie said. "But that's why I need your help! Please join our baking club!"

This time, Lexi looked up. "A club?" she asked.

"Yes, a baking club! It'll be awesome!" She thought this was just what Lexi needed—a support system. Friends to stand by her so she wouldn't be so shy and nervous all the time.

Lexi thought for a moment—then nodded. Kylie wasn't quite sure if that was a yes or a no, but she was hoping for the best. Two down, one more to go!

8

Slam Dunk

Kylie dreaded gym class—mostly because she felt like she was the slowest, clumsiest person on her team. Honestly, she didn't know where that came from. Her mom had been a tennis champ in high school, and her dad had been on the swim team and ran track. She couldn't even walk sometimes without getting her feet tangled up. And there was just something about the pressure of competition. Even if she knew how to shoot a basket or hit a softball, when all eyes were on her, she inevitably did the wrong thing.

Mr. Cangiano, the P.E. teacher, blew his whistle. "Give me twenty jumping jacks!" he shouted at the two fourth-grade classes gathered in the gymnasium. Kylie did her best, trying to jump high in the air and keep up with the count.

"Miss Carson," Mr. C. called. Oh no, thought Kylie, he knows my name! Teachers only knew your name if you were really good or really bad—and Kylie had a feeling she hadn't wowed him with her physical abilities.

"Let's see a little more arm action!"

Kylie waved her arms wildly in the air. "Like this?" She huffed and puffed.

She heard giggling behind her. "I can demonstrate if you like," Meredith offered. "My gymnastics coach makes me do one hundred jumping jacks to warm up for my meets."

"You think you can give us a hundred?" Mr. C. asked, scratching his head. He couldn't figure out if Meredith was bluffing or not. "Okay, let's see it." Meredith shoved past Kylie and the class began to chant: "1-2-3-4-5…"

Kylie couldn't believe it. Meredith looked so effortless.

"Show-off," someone grumbled. Kylie turned around and saw it was Sadie Harris, looking bored. Sadie was tall—really tall—like a full head taller than most fourth graders, which made her the best basketball player in P.E. She could shoot better than any boy—even her two older brothers, one of whom was a high-school football star.

The rumor (thanks to Meredith) was that Sadie was so tall because she was older than everyone in fourth grade. She should have been in fifth grade, but she was "held back." Kylie didn't know if that was true, but she did notice that Sadie struggled in class. When they were in third grade together, she sometimes she misread words or equations, and she worked with a special teacher in the library after school. Many of the kids teased Sadie and called her "Dummy" behind her back.

"...98-99-100!" Meredith wasn't even out of breath when she finished. She bowed to the crowd.

"Very impressive, Miss Mitchell," Mr. C. said, giving her a high five. "Now, kids, time to hit the hoops."

Kylie was on the blue team, and Jeremy Saperstone was the captain. Today they were pitted against the yellow team, headed by Sadie. Kylie saw Meredith pull on a yellow vest and give Sadie a nasty look. Meredith always wanted to be in charge.

"Hey, Kylie." Jeremy tapped her on the shoulder. "If you get the ball, just throw it to me, okay?"

"Um, okay," Kylie replied. Frankly, she hoped no one threw the ball in her direction at all. She wasn't very good at dribbling either. Mr. C. was always blowing his whistle at her for traveling, which meant she walked or ran with the ball instead of bouncing it.

When the clock started, Kylie found herself standing smack dab in the middle of a pack of running kids. She didn't have the slightest idea which way she was supposed to go.

"Over here! Over here!" Jeremy shouted. Kylie looked in his direction, then realized he wasn't talking to her.

"Move, Miss Carson!" called Mr. C. "Defense! Defense!" Kylie did her best to block the opposing team. But as she was running, she tripped and slid across the waxy wood floor, knocking Meredith down like a bowling pin.

Meredith quickly got to her feet, her hands raised in two tight fists. But Mr. C. stepped in to referee: "Yellow, your ball." He held it out to Meredith, and she grabbed it.

For the rest of the game, Kylie tried to just stay out of the way. Sadie managed to sink almost every basket, and the yellow team was leading 10 points to 6.

"Let's get some baskets!" Jeremy said. But a boy on the yellow team already had the ball and was dribbling right for Kylie. She put her arms up in front of her face and hoped he wouldn't run her over. Suddenly the ball slipped out of his fingers and landed at her feet.

"Pick it up!" screamed Jeremy. "Throw it here! I'm open!"

Kylie scooped up the ball and threw it with all her might at Jeremy. Instead it fell short, bouncing right off Meredith's head and into Sadie's hands.

"Thanks for the ball!" Sadie called. "Nice throw!"

Meredith was fuming. She stamped over to Kylie.

"You did that on purpose!" she yelled. "You tried to hit me."

"I didn't, honest," said Kylie. "It was an accident!"

Sadie sank the ball and the yellow team cheered. "At least your team got the point," Kylie said, trying to calm Meredith down.

"You're a freak!" Meredith snapped and stormed back to her side of the court, where Team Yellow was celebrating its victory.

Just what Kylie needed: another reason for Meredith to be mad at her. And her team wasn't very happy either. Jeremy just shook his head and looked annoyed.

At least Sadie was happy. She dribbled over to thank Kylie. "Sweet shot off Meredith's big head," she laughed. Kylie pictured Meredith's face, beet red with anger, and had to laugh herself. It *was* a pretty sweet shot!

Sweet! Kylie had almost forgotten about her baking club. "Hey, Sadie, can I ask you something?"

Sadie was still busy dribbling. "Yeah?"

"I'm starting this baking club after school on Wednesdays, and I thought maybe you'd want to join. It's going to be really cool."

Sadie stopped, held the ball under her arm, and scratched

her curly brown hair with her free hand. "Um, what would I have to do for it?"

"Nothing! We're going to learn how to make cakes and cookies and stuff. It'll be fun."

Sadie spun the ball on her fingertip. "I'm really not into stuff like that—you know baking and hair and makeup."

Kylie looked at what Sadie was wearing: a pair of sweat-pants, a Mets shirt, and a pair of running sneakers. She got it: she had to convince Sadie that baking wasn't just for girls.

"Did you ever hear of *The House of Wax*?" she asked her.

"Huh? No. What's that?" Sadie replied.

"Only one of the creepiest horror movies of all time. And *The Pit and the Pendulum*. Oh, and *The Masque of the Red Death*!"

"Sounds cool." Sadie stopped spinning her ball to listen.

"Well, they all starred this amazing monster-movie actor, Vincent Price. He was actually the narrator in the 'Thriller' video too." Kylie cleared her throat and did her best spooky-voice impression: "Darkness falls across the land…"

Sadie's eyes widened. "Oh yeah! I know that guy!"

"Well, Vincent Price—besides being an incredibly scary dude and the King of Horror—happened to be a gourmet chef."

"No kidding?" Sadie said.

"Seriously. He wrote a cookbook and everything." For once, Kylie's encyclopedic knowledge of monster movies was coming in handy.

Sadie went back to dribbling the ball in and out of her legs, and Kylie thought for a moment she'd lost her. Then Sadie asked, "There's like no test or anything to get into your club, right?"

"No way! You don't even have to know anything about baking."

Sadie took a shot from mid-court, and it landed with a *swoosh* right in the basket. "I guess it would be okay. I don't really get to do much after school except practice basketball and work with tutors and stuff."

"Perfect! See you tomorrow! We're meeting in the teachers' lounge," Kylie chirped. That was it—she had her four members! She couldn't wait to tell Juliette and, even more, to start coming up with mouthwatering recipes for the club to bake. She was so happy that she forgot all about the P.E. disaster—and luckily Meredith had hip-hop club after school and wasn't on her bus home to torture her.

☆ ☮ ☆

When the bus dropped her off at home, Kylie practically floated through the door.

"Well, someone's in a great mood," said her mom, as Kylie skipped around the living room. "Care to tell me why?"

"You're looking at the first president of the Blakely Elementary School baking club," Kylie beamed.

"Wow, that's great, honey!" said her mom. "Were you elected?"

"Sort of. More like chosen by my teacher. And I recruited all the members myself. First meeting is tomorrow after school."

"Well, good for you!" replied her mom, giving her a hug. "I'm very proud."

That night, after she finished her social studies and math homework, Kylie pored over her mom's cookbooks, putting Post-its on dozens of recipes that seemed simply scrumptious: crème brûlée, tiramisu, pumpkin tart with anise-seed crust, frozen lemon gingersnap pie. Each one sounded more delicious than the one before it. She took a blank composition notebook out of her desk and wrote "Cupcake Club" with a purple Sharpie on the cover. It made her feel very official. On page 1 she made a list of her goals:

1.   Bake something new and yummy every week.
2.   Get kids at school to like me.
3.   Get Meredith to stop hating me.

She thought for a second, chewing on her pencil eraser, then added:

4.   Make $ selling treats at a bake sale so I can buy a cool phone!

She hadn't started the club to make money, but why not? When she lived in Jupiter, she and her mom had always organized bake sales for her Brownie troop and sold pitchers of lemonade on their lawn in the summer. Her dad liked to say, "Smart business and money go hand in hand." She supposed he was talking about his accounting clients, but why couldn't she be a smart businesswoman too?

Smart businesswomen needed to dress the part, so Kylie rummaged through her closet and dresser drawers, trying to find the perfect first-day baking-club outfit. She tried on a jean skirt and a navy sweater. Business-like but too boring, she thought. Then she remembered: the pink shirt her gram Bobbi had sent her for Valentine's Day the year before. On it were a sparkly cupcake and the words "Life is Sweet!"

At the time, Kylie had thought the shirt was a little babyish and she'd buried it in the bottom of her drawer. But now it seemed just perfect: bright, cheerful, and optimistic—and she loved the sweet message. She'd wear it with her best black pleated skirt, the one she wore to her cousin Zoe's bat mitzvah, and a pair of cute black boots.

Her mom poked her head in Kylie's bedroom door and noticed the clothes scattered on her bed—as well as all over the floor.

"Did a cyclone sweep through here?" her mom asked.

"Just trying out outfits for my first baking-club meeting," Kylie explained. "I'll clean it up. Promise."

Her mom nodded. "I thought you might need something for your meeting." She pulled a small wrapped present from behind her back.

"For me? Thanks!" Kylie ripped off the wrapping paper. It was a tube of pearly lip gloss.

"This is awesome!" she said, hugging her mom.

"I was saving it for Chanukah—but I thought it was perfect for you now. The color is called Pink Frosting."

Kylie opened the tube and slicked some on her lips. She looked in her mirror and saw that it gave her smile a delicate pink shine. And it tasted like buttercream frosting!

"Are you all ready for your big meeting?" her mom asked.

"I think so," Kylie replied. "I think I just need to borrow a few things."

Her mom raised an eyebrow. "What do you mean *borrow*?"

Kylie went into the kitchen and began pulling stuff out of the utensil drawer. "Like this spatula—that would be great. Ooh! This cool whisk! We could use that for making meringue!" When she was finished, dozens of baking tools, a hand mixer, and a mini chopper were spread out on the kitchen counter. She wasn't sure how much the school kitchen had—or what Juliette was bringing. So just to be sure…

"Well, I guess with this big freelance writing project I have to work on, I won't have much time for baking…or chopping," her mom sighed. "Okay, you can borrow them. But honestly, Kylie, I think you're better off starting small. One cake at a time?"

"Don't you and Daddy always tell me to dream big?"

"Yes, we do. And you've definitely made a *big* mess of my kitchen and your bedroom." She handed Kylie a wooden spoon. "Start packing it up, Madam President."

☆ ☮ ☆

Wednesday at school, Kylie could barely concentrate in class. All she could think about was the club meeting at 3:15 p.m. When Ms. Shottlan asked her to name the fiftieth state to join the Union, she accidentally blurted out, "Pineapple upside-down cake!" Her teacher looked puzzled as the class giggled.

"I mean, Hawaii," Kylie said, trying to cover. "You know, Hawaii has lots of pineapples? It's kind of my trick for remembering it." She hoped everyone was buying this lame explanation.

"Okay," Ms. Shottlan replied. "Hawaii, home of pineapples, is correct."

Science class went even worse. "What do plants contain that makes them green?" asked Mr. Reidy.

Kylie was busy daydreaming about whipping up the perfect buttercream frosting, stirring in the butter, the milk…

"Kylie?" Mr. Reidy caught her off guard.

"Sugar!" Kylie answered.

The class roared with laughter—especially Meredith, whose hand shot up. "Ooh, I know! Mr. Reidy, I know! It's chlorophyll."

Kylie tried to focus for the rest of the class, but she found herself watching the hands on the wall clock tick down to the last period bell. Finally, at exactly 3 p.m. it rang, and she raced back to her classroom closet to pull out two tote bags filled with baking tools and cookbooks. She dragged them down the hall to the teachers' lounge and struggled to open the door with both hands full.

"I've got it," said Jenna, helping her inside. Kylie was thrilled to see her—and the other girls as well. They had all come, just as they promised. She rested her bags on the kitchen counter and heaved a sigh of relief.

"I'm really glad you guys are here!" she said.

Jenna peeked into the bags. "So what are we baking?"

"Um, I have lots of ideas," Kylie began.

"Yeah, but what ingredients did you bring?" asked Sadie.

"Ingredients?" Kylie couldn't believe that with all her planning, she'd forgotten the most important thing of all: the stuff the club needed to actually bake!

"Well, I thought we'd kind of talk about what we want to make—you know, plan it out?"

Lexi shook her head—and Jenna dug into her backpack, pulling out a candy bar. "I thought the purpose of a baking club was to bake," she said with a mouthful of caramel. "Lame."

"Seriously lame!" Sadie chimed in.

Just then, Juliette walked in, and Kylie had never been so glad to see anyone in her life!

"Hey, girls—ready to get bakin'?"

Kylie whispered in her ear, "Small problem. I kind of forgot to bring ingredients."

Juliette smiled and whispered back, "I kind of didn't forget—no sweat!"

Phew! Kylie felt like hugging Juliette for saving the day. Their teacher unloaded flour, butter, sugar, and a bunch of other ingredients onto the counter.

"Before we begin, I think Kylie should explain a little about what this club is," Juliette said. "Kylie, take it away!"

Kylie gulped and flipped through her notebook. Nowhere in all the plans that she'd written down did she include a speech! She sent Juliette a telepathic "SOS!" but her adviser just smiled and gave her a thumbs-up sign.

"Well, this club is about baking," Kylie began.

"Obviously!" chuckled Jenna.

"And it's also about us working together," Kylie continued.

"Like a team?" asked Sadie.

"Exactly! We're a team. Everyone will have a job to do, and everyone's opinion is important."

The girls nodded. Kylie relaxed a little. "I want this to be really fun and cool," she added. "I was looking forward to it all day, and I hope you guys were too." Kylie saw Lexi shrug and Jenna yawn. This was not the enthusiasm she had hoped for.

"Baking is amazing," Kylie said. "It's like a wizard creating magic! You start with a few ingredients and *poof*! After a few minutes in the oven, it all comes together into a delicious dessert."

"If you do it right," cautioned Juliette. "You have to follow directions very precisely in baking."

Well, that was true. One time she and her mom had decided to "wing" a fudge brownie recipe instead of following the one in the cookbook. Why couldn't they add an entire can of cocoa powder? The more chocolate the better, right? Instead it stuck to the bottom of the pan and tasted like bitter, burnt hot cocoa.

Then there was the cheesecake she'd made for her dad's birthday. Kylie was so excited to serve it that she didn't let it set long enough in the fridge, and it came out like cheesecake soup! Juliette was right. If you didn't pay attention to the recipe, it never turned out the way it was supposed to.

Sadie frowned. "Baking sounds hard."

"Sounds like a Harry Potter spell," Jenna snickered.

"The best way to learn is by doing," Juliette said. "I was thinking maybe something simple for starters—like chocolate-chip muffins."

"I like chocolate-chip muffins!" said Jenna.

"Yeah," said Sadie. "They're pretty good."

Lexi nodded her approval.

"Then what are we waiting for?" asked Juliette. She dug into her bag and handed each of the girls a purple apron to tie around their waists.

"My favorite color!" Kylie exclaimed. "Cool!"

"Well, I thought we needed to look like an official club," Juliette said. "And basic chef's white seemed a little stuffy—I thought we'd be a little more colorful." The girls nodded in approval. "Ladies, put on your aprons and let's get started!"

Juliette placed the recipe on the Smart Board projector and Kylie skimmed the instructions. "For little muffins, these look pretty complicated," she said. "Are you sure we're going to be able to make these?"

"You never know till you try," Juliette said, preheating the oven to 350 degrees.

Jenna assembled all the ingredients on the counter: flour, sugar, baking powder, milk, oil, eggs, salt, vanilla, and a bowl of chocolate chips. She tasted a chip. "Mmmm…semi-sweet, I'd say."

"Ding! Ding! Ding! You are correct!" laughed Juliette. "You know your chocolate."

"Mix together all the dry ingredients," Kylie read. "Lexi, hand me 2 cups of flour. And Sadie, how much sugar do we need?"

Sadie glanced at the Smart Board and looked confused. "Um, 2½ cups?" She poured the sugar into the measuring cup.

"I'll crack the eggs," offered Jenna. Kylie noticed she got several pieces of shell in the batter and was trying to fish them out.

Juliette watched the girls work, not offering a single comment or suggestion. Kylie wished Juliette would jump in every now and then, because none of them had any idea what they were doing! But she was the president, so she would have to lead them.

"Okay, fire up the mixer," she instructed Lexi.

Lexi clicked the switch to 8 and the flour went flying! Everything had a coating of white powder.

"Slower! Slower!" Kylie shouted over the roaring paddle. "Put it on 2."

The mixer slowed and quieted down. All four girls peered into the bowl, watching the ingredients blend into a yellow blob.

"This is going to take forever," Jenna moaned. "I'm starving!"

"It says to add the chocolate chips once the wet and dry ingredients are smoothly combined," Kylie said.

"It doesn't look very smooth to me," Lexi finally piped up. Huge clumps of butter were stuck to the blades of the mixer and the sides of the bowl. "Shouldn't we scrape this into the mixture?"

"It's fine, it's fine," Kylie replied. Then she dumped the entire bowl of chocolate chips into the batter. They mixed the batter for several more minutes and observed that it was now a brown, polka-dotted liquid.

"I don't think you're supposed to make a smoothie out of it," Sadie sighed. "It says not to overbeat."

"It's okay," said Kylie. "Once we get it baked, you'll never know."

Using ice-cream scoopers, they filled muffin pans with the batter.

"I like big muffins," said Jenna. "These cups look tiny. Make sure you fill them to the top."

"But it says fill two-thirds of the way," Lexi pointed out.

"Oh, it's close enough," Jenna insisted. The batter spilled over the cups and all over the pan, and as they placed it in the oven, half of the batter sloshed onto the floor and on the oven door.

They needed to wait 30 minutes for the timer to ring. Juliette suggested they go around the group and each say their favorite treat. Kylie pulled out her notebook to take notes. "This way, I can look up the recipes and we can make one each week."

"I love these apricot wheat-germ muffins my mom makes before a game," said Sadie.

Jenna made a face. "Eww, that's really gross! Wheat germ?"

"It's healthy," Sadie protested. "Okay, fine—banana bran loaf."

"Bran?" Jenna pretended to gag. "Remind me to miss that week's meeting."

"Well, what do *you* want to make?" asked Sadie.

"My madre's *torrijas*."

"Translation?" Kylie asked, jotting it down in her book.

"It's like bread pudding—made with milk, sugar, eggs, and sweet honey."

"Sounds good," Kylie replied. "What about you, Lexi?"

Lexi thought for a minute. "Rainbow marzipan cookies," she answered softly. "I love the colors."

"Now your turn, Kylie," said Sadie. "You have a lot of cookbooks there—what's your favorite?"

"That's a tough one," Kylie said, chewing her pen cap. "I guess I'd have to say Death by Chocolate."

Sadie gulped. "You want to bake something that kills us?"

"No, it's a cake," groaned Jenna. "A really rich cake."

"My aunt Peggy makes it for birthdays with rich chocolate-pudding filling and shaved chocolate flakes on top," Kylie explained.

"All this talking about desserts is making me hungry," moaned Jenna. "How much longer do we have to wait for these muffins to be done?"

"Three minutes," replied Juliette. The girls gathered impatiently around the window of the oven door. Finally the timer dinged.

Juliette took out the pan and placed it on the counter. The muffins looked sad and sunken—not to mention a little burnt around the edges.

"I don't get it! What happened?" Jenna asked.

"Well, let's see," said Juliette. "Let's go over everything you did."

The girls listed all the ingredients they had placed in the bowl. Then Lexi noticed a small red-and-yellow can in the corner. "Baking powder?" she said, pointing to the can. "I think we forgot this."

"Which explains why the muffins didn't rise," said Juliette.

"Can we taste one anyway?" asked Jenna. "I don't care if mine is a little flat."

She popped a warm crumb in her mouth…then spit it out. "Yuck! This is so sweet it's disgusting! Sadie, how much sugar is in here?"

"I did what the recipe said," Sadie replied, crossing her arms over her chest. "It's not my fault."

"How many cups did the recipe call for?" asked Juliette. Sadie tried to recall. "Um, 2½."

"What? That says 1½!" yelled Jenna, looking at the Smart Board. "Can't you read?"

"I can read," Sadie protested. "I just must have been in a hurry." She looked at the baking pan and sighed, "I'm really sorry I ruined everything."

For a moment, Kylie was worried Sadie was going to cry. "Look, it's not all your fault, Sadie. I beat the batter too much and put in way too many chocolate chips. I'm just as much to blame as you are."

Jenna spit a broken eggshell into her hand. "Yeah, me too. I don't think these muffins were supposed to have a hard crunch."

Sadie nodded. "It's just that sometimes my brain sees things in the wrong order."

"What do you mean?" asked Jenna.

"It's called dyslexia. I'm not stupid. I have a learning disorder."

"Oh," said Jenna softly. "We didn't know."

"No," Sadie replied. "Not a lot of people do. It's kind of embarrassing, you know?"

"That's okay, Sadie," Juliette patted her on the back. "People make mistakes. But we've learned a valuable lesson today."

"That we stink as bakers?" asked Kylie.

"No, that baking is a science. You have to follow the ingredients and the instructions exactly until you are comfortable, confident, and skilled enough to improvise."

"I don't ever see that happening," Kylie muttered.

"It will happen, I promise. And here's the most important thing: you guys make a great team. I watched you all working together. Nobody was bossy, and nobody was lazy. It was a real group effort. You're going to be a great club. It's your first time. Cut yourselves some slack!"

Kylie looked at their inedible muffins and the mess all over the kitchen. Batter, flour, and dirty bowls were everywhere. "We should clean up," she sighed.

"I'll wash," said Sadie.

"I'll dry," said Jenna.

Lexi grabbed a broom and started to sweep.

Well, thought Kylie, maybe Juliette was right. They all did pitch in when it counted. She stood up and dumped the muffins into the garbage.

The girls started laughing.

"What's so funny?" Kylie asked.

"You have batter all over your butt!" giggled Jenna, pointing. "We must have gotten some on the stool and you sat in it."

Kylie felt her face flush. If this had happened in front of Meredith, she would have been mortified. She would have run off to the bathroom or ducked for cover. But somehow here, in front of her club, in front of these girls, it didn't bother her quite so much. She turned around, shook her butt in the air, and cracked up. "Look, it's the Batter Butt Dance!"

Jenna and Sadie joined in, bumping their hips together and strutting around the room. Lexi watched from the corner, smiling, and then began wiggling around as she swept the floor. "Go, Lexi! Go, Lexi!" the girls chanted.

Lexi looked embarrassed. Kylie quickly made a time-out sign with her hands. "Jenna, Sadie…stop!" she shushed them. "Sorry, Lexi!" She was afraid Lexi would run out of the room and never come back again.

But instead Lexi took a deep breath, dropped the broom, and shook her butt at them.

"You go, girl!" Sadie said, high-fiving her.

Kylie made up a rap: "It's a mess—but don't stress! The baking club's a big success! Take a chance and do the Batter Butt Dance!"

They danced and sang as they cleaned. They were having so much fun that they didn't even mind the work.

"Nice job, ladies," said Juliette. "Everything is spick-and-span."

"See you all next Wednesday?" Kylie asked as they turned off the lights and closed the door to the teachers' lounge behind them. She held her breath, waiting for them to answer.

"Yeah," Sadie said, and Jenna and Lexi nodded. "See ya."

9

Starting from Scratch

The next week was, as Sadie so perfectly put it, "a whole different ball game" for the Blakely baking club. First of all, Kylie came prepared with five copies of a simple vanilla cupcake recipe and all the ingredients. The girls carefully reviewed the recipe together before they began baking and discussed who would handle what task.

"Yum, Madagascar vanilla," said Jenna, sampling a drop of the extract Kylie had brought. Kylie picked up the bottle—it just said "Pure Vanilla Extract." But when she looked at the fine print on the label, sure enough, the vanilla was from Madagascar. "Jenna, you are amazing, and I am appointing you our official taste tester!" Kylie exclaimed.

Lexi would be in charge of piping the frosting onto the cupcakes in an artistic swirl.

"Watch this," said Sadie, cracking an egg meticulously into the bowl with one hand.

Jenna peered into the bowl. "How do you do that?" she marveled. "Not a single splinter of eggshell!"

Sadie shrugged. "I'm good at handling a softball—an egg is just smaller." So Sadie was in charge of all cracking.

Kylie put herself on mixer duty. She'd make sure that the ingredients were perfectly combined in just the right order on just the right speed. This time when they checked the batter, it had a lovely creamy color and consistency—and smelled delicious.

"It says bake for 17 to 25 minutes," said Kylie. "I guess that means they're not so sure how long it will take."

"It means every oven and every cupcake batter is different," explained Juliette. She demonstrated how they could insert a toothpick into the cupcakes to see if they were done. "If it comes out clean, you are good to go."

This time when they scooped the batter into the muffin cups, they were careful not to overfill them: two-thirds of the way was just the right amount. And they wiped off any splatters on the pan so the cupcakes wouldn't come out with crusty, burnt edges.

The cupcakes took exactly 21 minutes to bake to perfection. Juliette suggested they let them cool for another 15 minutes and discuss what kind of icing design they wanted to create. Jenna mixed confectioners' sugar and butter with a tablespoon of vanilla to create a delicately sweet buttercream frosting, and Lexi added a few drops of red food coloring to turn it a rosy shade of pink.

"Pretty!" Kylie exclaimed. "Lexi, you really are an artist!" She watched as Lexi piped tiny swirls around the edge of the cupcake, ending with a dollop in the center. When she was finished, the icing looked like the petals of a flower.

"Wow!" Sadie and Jenna both gasped. "Awesome!"

"But the real test of a cupcake is how it tastes," said Juliette. "Everyone dig in."

They each took a bite.

"Delicioso!" declared Jenna. "Absolutely heaven!"

"This is amazing," said Kylie. "I have never tasted such a yummy cupcake."

"I agree," said Juliette. "As good as Gram Gaga's! It's moist, it's light, it's flavorful. The frosting isn't too sweet or too sticky. A 10! Ladies, cupcakes are definitely your thing."

"Then that's what we should bake," said Kylie. "Just cupcakes. Perfect, beautiful, delicious cupcakes—like no one has ever tasted before."

"A cupcake club?" asked Jenna. "That's kinda cool."

"We need a name for it," said Sadie, licking her fingers.

"Like the Blakely Bears is the name of our basketball team. Every team has to have an awesome name."

Kylie nodded. "How about the Cupcake Queens?"

Sadie winced. "I am so not into princesses."

"The Cupcake Crusaders?" Jenna offered. Lexi gave it a thumbs-down. "Sounds like a superhero," she said. "What about the Blakely Bakers?"

The girls winced.

"Why don't you try this?" said Juliette. "What qualities do you want your club to embody? What should it represent? Who should belong to it?"

"No liars, bullies, or phonies," Kylie replied.

"It's about treating each other with respect," said Sadie. "It's about being a good friend *and* a good baker."

"And don't forget the cupcakes," said Jenna, sampling a second.

Kylie thought hard. The purple peace sign she had doodled on her notebook cover gave her a great idea. "It's about Peace…Love…and Cupcakes: PLC."

Jenna, Lexi, and Sadie stared. "That's it!" said Jenna. "That's exactly it! Kylie, that's perfect!"

Lexi quickly sketched a pink cupcake on a sheet of paper with the words "Peace, Love, and Cupcakes" written across the wrapper. On the frosting, she drew a purple peace sign. "Our logo," she smiled.

"Cool!" the girls gushed.

"Now that you have a name for your club, there's only one thing left to do," said Juliette. "Let's get your fabulous cupcakes out for everyone to taste. And I have the perfect way to do it."

10

The Eco-licious Cupcake

As soon as Principal Fontina unveiled the plans for an eco center to be constructed on the roof of Blakely Elementary, the entire school began buzzing with excitement. Blakely would be the first school in Connecticut to have such a facility. There would be an outdoor classroom and a huge garden filled with fruits, vegetables, and herbs.

"It's going to be amazing," Kylie told her mom. "With a weather station, a greenhouse, even a turtle pond. Principal Fontina says we'll be able to grow real food and spices to use in the cafeteria lunches!"

What Kylie was most excited about was the state-of-the-art laboratory that would be housed in the eco center. She imagined herself watching over a steaming beaker and pouring mixtures into test tubes, just like in Dr. Frankenstein's lab. Maybe she'd create a bug that was part fly, part spider...or a plant that could sing, like the one in *Little Shop of Horrors*.

"Can you just imagine what amazing carrot or zucchini cupcakes our club will be able to make with what we grow in the garden?" Kylie said.

"It does sound amazing," said her mother. "But something like that must also be very expensive."

That was just the problem: the school needed to raise money—a lot of money—to build the eco center. So Principal Fontina had organized an Eco Fair and asked each school club to come up with an activity or product to sell to benefit the eco center. Juliette suggested that Peace, Love, and Cupcakes create something in the spirit of the fair—an "eco-licious" cupcake.

"Let's use organic ingredients," Sadie said.

"Dark chocolate," said Jenna. "It has to be dark chocolate. And I'm thinking a chocolate ganache icing. I saw it on the Food Channel. Yum! It'll be super rich."

"What's ganache?" Lexi asked.

"It's a mixture of chocolate and cream that you melt together," Jenna explained. "It looks really shiny."

"I could do decorations that look like the Earth," suggested Lexi. "I've seen the *Cake Boss* guy use different colors of fondant—it's this gum paste that you can shape and mold like Play-Doh."

88

"Great! And let's use recycled paper wrappers," added Kylie. "This is really going to wow everyone."

"You all have great ideas," said Juliette. "But I think we should do a test run. Ganache can be tricky."

"But they said on TV it's really simple," said Jenna. "There are only two ingredients."

"I think we learned our lesson from the chocolate-chip-muffin mess-up," said Kylie. "Practice makes perfect."

The girls gathered in the club kitchen and read the directions carefully. "It says to chop the chocolate into small pieces," said Jenna.

"You want to be really careful with your fingers," Juliette explained, opening an organic chocolate bar and taking a large knife from the kitchen drawer. "And always make sure you have adult supervision."

"Yeah," giggled Kylie. "Blood and guts are for horror movies, not cupcakes."

The girls watched as Juliette demonstrated how to hold the knife by the handle and above the blade so the chocolate flaked off in delicate thin slices. "If the chocolate pieces are too big, they won't melt evenly," Juliette advised.

While Juliette filled a bowl with chocolate shavings, Sadie turned the flame on under the saucepan to heat the cream. They were all busy sampling the chocolate crumbs when something made a loud hissing sound.

"Oh no!" screamed Sadie, racing to turn off the stove. The cream was boiling over. "How did that happen?"

"Oops," said Kylie. "It says to remove it from the heat immediately once it boils." The floor was now puddled with cream, and there was hardly anything left in the saucepan. "We'll have to do it again."

Sadie started from scratch and this time watched the pot carefully. Once the cream had boiled, the recipe said to pour it over the chocolate. Kylie whisked the mixture.

"Is it supposed to look like this?" she asked. "I thought ganache was smooth. This looks sticky and gross." She held up the whisk, and the chocolate stuck to it in large clumps—like the time she'd blown a bubble and gotten gum stuck in her hair.

"Keep stirring," said Juliette. "It will get darker and smoother."

"We'll take turns," suggested Lexi.

Each of the girls whisked the mixture until their hands ached. Finally it turned into a shiny liquid.

Jenna peered into the saucepan. "No more lumps." She smiled. "It's ready!"

Kylie brought out the tray of organic chocolate cupcakes that had baked and cooled. "Now what? How do we get the ganache on the cupcakes?"

Lexi picked up a large pastry brush and dipped it in the warm chocolate. She began painting a cupcake, then stepped back to observe her work. "It doesn't look smooth," she said. "I can see the texture of the brushstrokes."

"I saw them make a chocolate torte on TV, and they poured the chocolate over the top of the cake," suggested Jenna. She picked up the bowl and poured the chocolate on top of a cupcake.

"Well, that works—but that's way too much ganache," Kylie said. "I don't think you're supposed to drown the cupcake."

Sadie had another suggestion. "When in doubt, dip!" she said. "My brothers dip everything in ketchup: chicken nuggets, fries, even waffles." She tried to dip the top of a cupcake in the chocolate, but it slipped from her fingers and fell into the bowl.

"Oh no!" Sadie yelped, trying to fish it out of the sea of chocolate. It kept sinking further and further under.

"Let me help," said Jenna. Soon she was up to her wrists in chocolate too.

Kylie handled them a ladle. "Try this," she suggested. The cupcake came out easily in the spoon, and Jenna and Sadie licked their fingers clean.

"If you dip, you have to do it slowly and carefully," Juliette explained. She demonstrated how to roll the cupcake from side to side in the ganache, coating it evenly.

The girls practiced, dipping a dozen and placing each cupcake on a tray lined with wax paper. Then they let the cupcakes cool and set for 15 minutes. The chocolate formed a smooth, glossy glaze.

Jenna was the first to sample their creation. "Not bad, if I do say so myself," she said. "We might need to put on a little thicker coat of chocolate, though—for chocoholics like me. Maybe double dip?"

"Sure," said Kylie. But as she went to dip a naked cupcake in chocolate for practice, she noticed the ganache had completely stiffened and now had a thick gooey texture.

"Hey, what happened?" she asked.

"The ganache has to stay warm," Juliette explained. "You might have to boil a pot of water and keep the chocolate in a bowl on top of it. Especially if you're working with a lot of cupcakes. And for the Eco Fair, we're going to need a *lot* of cupcakes."

☆ ☮ ☆

The day of the Eco Fair, each club set up a booth in the school gymnasium. The track team sold tie-dyed shoe-laces and bandanas. The math team sold green rulers that read, "Eco Kids Rule!" And Meredith's hip-hop club was selling a video.

"It's an original dance routine I choreographed," Meredith announced. "It's called, 'It's Easy Being Green.'" She was dressed head to toe in green, from her sequin-trimmed sweater to her ruffled miniskirt. Even her ballet shoes were the color of a dill pickle. And she held a green bedazzled microphone as she rapped the lyrics: "I can, I can, I can recycle cans." Then she did a cartwheel and landed in a split.

"Wow, just looking at her makes me want to puke," whispered Sadie.

Kylie giggled. "Just wait till she gets a taste of our cup-cakes. She'll be *green* with envy!"

"I don't think she could get much greener," chuckled Jenna.

Juliette and Lexi wheeled in a table with PLC's amazing display: a huge papier-mâché cupcake "tree" centerpiece with the Eco-licious Cupcakes perched in the branches and all around the trunk. The crowd made a beeline for the table.

"I just have a few more finishing touches," said Lexi, sprinkling edible luster dust on the fondant Earths to give them a magical shimmer. "There!"

"It's a masterpiece!" said Kylie, hugging Lexi.

"I'll say," said a deep British accent behind them. A large man with a mustache and a bowler hat was the first in line. "May I buy one?"

"Sure!" said Kylie. "That'll be $5 for the eco center."

The man was dressed in a dark brown suit, almost the same color as the dark chocolate in their recipe. He took a huge bite, closed his eyes, and savored the taste for several minutes. Every now and then, he'd mumble, "Mmm, mmm, mmm." Kylie giggled at how much he seemed to enjoy every morsel.

But he wasn't the only fan. The PLC booth was swarming with people who wanted to buy cupcakes, some even seconds and thirds.

"These cupcakes are really spectacular," said Principal Fontina. She was licking her fingers. "If this is just the first thing your club baked, I can't wait to see what you come up with next."

Kylie noticed out of the corner of her eye that the man in the chocolate-brown suit was watching them.

"What's with him?" she whispered to Jenna.

"I dunno. I heard him ask Mr. Reidy and Ms. Bayder if they liked the cupcakes."

"Do you think he's like the Baking Police or something?" asked Sadie. "Did we do something wrong?"

"The Baking Police? *Really?*" Jenna groaned. "There's no such thing. And we did everything right—which is why these are selling like hotcakes, not cupcakes."

Just then, the man strolled over, pushing his way in front of a dozen people in line. Kylie gulped.

"May I have a word with you girls?" he began. "I've been watching you."

"See! I told you—the Baking Police!" Sadie whispered.

He reached into his pocket, and for a second Kylie was terrified he was about to pull out a badge...or handcuffs!

"My card," he said, handing it to Kylie. She looked down and read, "Louis Ludwig, *Owner and Connoisseur*, The Golden Spoon Gourmet Grocery." "I would like to speak to the pastry chef."

"I don't understand," said Kylie. "We're not in trouble?"

"Trouble? *Au contraire!* I own a fabulous gourmet shop

in Greenwich, and judging by how many people love your cupcakes, I must have them for my store. Now, girls, can you please direct me to the person responsible for these delectable cupcakes? I am a busy man. I don't have all day to dillydally."

"Well, that would be us," said Kylie, proudly. "We baked the cupcakes."

Mr. Ludwig chuckled. "Surely you don't expect me to believe that four little girls made these?"

"Hey, watch who you're calling little girls," Jenna said.

"I just simply cannot believe it!" said Mr. Ludwig.

"Now you're calling us liars too?" cried Jenna. She turned to Kylie and whispered, "I don't think I like this dude. He's a snob!"

"We're really the bakers," Kylie assured him. "Our club is called Peace, Love, and Cupcakes. We wouldn't lie! We worked really hard on this recipe!"

"Well, in that case, I would like to hire your club to make twenty dozen of these for me for Monday morning."

"Twenty dozen?" gasped Kylie. "That's 240 cupcakes!"

"Precisely!" replied the man. "I am willing to pay you $2.50 a cupcake. Monday by 8 a.m. I open at 8:30, and I will not take no for an answer. Simply scrumptious!" He polished off another cupcake and handed Kylie two $100 bills in advance to pay for the ingredients. Then he marched away, brushing chocolate crumbs out of his mustache.

"I don't believe it," said Jenna. "So 240 cupcakes at $2.50 each…"

"Is $600," said Kylie. "From one customer! *OMG!*" She looked at the money in her hand. "I don't think I have ever held a $100 bill before."

"Can we bake that many cupcakes?" Lexi spoke up. She was picturing having to roll out and stamp 240 sparkly fondant Earths. Each tiny circle was made up of several different colors to look like a globe—and it had taken her hours to make a thin sheet of each color with a rolling pin and then cut out the shapes of the continents with an X-acto blade. "I mean, we only made 100 cupcakes for the Eco Fair, and that took us two days!"

"Well, we'll have to bake faster. And work harder," said Kylie. "And buy more ingredients. This is incredible."

☆ ☮ ☆

What was more incredible was how fast the cupcakes went at the Eco Fair—in two hours they had sold out entirely, and several customers were begging the girls to produce another tray.

"Sorry, everybody, we're totally sold out! Thank you so much!" said Kylie. A groan of disappointment swept through the crowd.

"I guess Mr. Ludwig was on to something," said Sadie. "These cupcakes are really popular, guys. Everyone wants more!"

Everyone except Meredith, who had stacks of DVDs still piled high on her table. She gave Kylie a dirty look, then headed right for PLC's booth.

"Look out, here comes trouble," snickered Jenna, as Meredith approached them.

Meredith stared at the club's sign over their booth. "PLC? What does that stand for? Pathetic Losers Club?"

Kylie gritted her teeth. "It stands for Peace, Love, and Cupcakes."

"Cupcakes? That's the best you could do?" Meredith sniffed. "Anyone can bake cupcakes."

"But not just anyone could make $1,100 selling their cupcakes," countered Kylie.

"Someone's a sore loser," said Sadie. "Face it, Meredith, we beat you."

"Really? That's funny, because I sold every one of our DVDs. All 200 of them, and at $10 each, that's

$2,000—which is more than you losers made. Toodles…I have to go tweet this."

Meredith skipped off, grinning. Kylie muttered, "I really, *really* don't like her."

"Her rich parents probably said they'd buy all the leftover DVDs," said Jenna. "Don't believe anything she says, Kylie."

"And don't let her spoil our great mood," added Sadie. "We did amazing today! Just think, if we really opened up a business, we could be rich!"

"And people really loved the cupcakes," added Juliette. "All we had left were a few crumbs—and Ms. Fine, the PTA president, was eating those too!"

"You're right," said Kylie. She straightened her shoulders and took a deep breath. She wasn't about to let Meredith distract her from the task at hand. "We have two days to bake 240 cupcakes and get them to Greenwich before school starts Monday morning!"

Sugar Rush

Kylie calculated that making 240 cupcakes would take them about three hours.

"How did you figure that out?" asked her mom, picturing her kitchen held hostage all Sunday afternoon by four junior cupcake chefs.

"Well, we can fit four trays of twelve cupcakes in the oven at a time, and each batch takes about twenty-five minutes. So that's forty-eight cupcakes every half hour. Plus time to let them cool and be decorated…"

"Uh, huh," replied her mom. "What time do the girls arrive?"

"I told them to come over at three and we'd be finished by dinnertime." She kissed her mom on the cheek. "I wouldn't want to miss taco night."

Lexi arrived first, carrying several bags and a large globe.

"What is all this?" asked Kylie.

"Well, I thought we should be more exact with our fondant Earths—you know, get the blue and the green just right? I felt like we rushed them for the Eco-licious Cupcakes, and my South America didn't really look like South America."

"It's great that you want it to be so perfect, Lex," said Kylie. "But I don't know if we'll have the time."

Kylie couldn't even argue, because Jenna was next at the house with her own packages.

"I brought us six different organic chocolates to choose from," she said. "I think we should make one batch with Swiss and one with Dutch and compare."

Sadie was right behind her, carrying two more bags of chocolate. "We also bought some Valrhona and Dakota."

Jenna corrected her. "Not Dakota, *Dagoba* chocolate. It's really premium stuff. Whole Foods had a ton of different kinds."

Kylie looked at all the groceries. "How much money did you guys spend?"

"Not that much," said Jenna, shuffling her feet. "Just $87."

"Plus the $36 on the recycled paper wrappers," added Sadie.

"And my $72 on fondant, luster dust, and a new rolling pin."

Kylie did some quick math in her head. "You guys spent $195! All we have left from the $200 Mr. Ludwig gave us is $5?"

"No, not $5," said Jenna. "$3. We bought a recycled tote bag for $1.99 to carry stuff in—save the Earth!"

Kylie rested her head in her hands. "Did we really need all this stuff?" she sighed. "I know it's fun to try new ingredients and make perfect fondant Earths, but we really can't spend money till we make money."

"Well, we are making money," said Sadie. "$600."

"Minus the $200 you guys just spent, that's only $400. And we'll need half of that to put back into the club treasury for our next baking project.

"We're sorry, Kylie," said Lexi. "I guess we got excited."

"And carried away," said Jenna. "But you really have to taste some of this chocolate."

Kylie gave up. There was no winning. At least the girls were really psyched to bake.

"Look on the bright side, Kylie," insisted Sadie as she unpacked the chocolate onto the kitchen counter. "Whatever we don't use now, we can use later."

Kylie pointed at Jenna, who was already opening up bars and sampling them. "Really?"

Jenna shrugged. "This is so delicious," she said, her mouth full of a Belgian bar. "You have to try this!" She held out the wrapper to Kylie, who took a tiny piece. The chocolate was so creamy, so delicate that it melted the minute it touched her lips.

"Wow, that is amazing," Kylie said. "So much for leftovers. I want another piece!"

Thanks to Jenna's experimenting (they baked five dozen batches before choosing the silky Belgian chocolate) and Lexi's exacting artwork (she was positive North America was pointier), it was just past midnight when Kylie gave the last cupcake a brushing of luster dust. They had been working for nine hours straight!

"There," she sighed. "That makes 250 cupcakes—not counting the three that Jenna ate, the one Kylie dropped…"

"And the one I ran over with my skateboard," said Sadie.

Kylie's parents poked their heads into the kitchen. "Girls, do you have any idea what time it is? And there's school tomorrow!" said her mom.

"We just have to box these up, Mom," Kylie said. "And, Dad, I need you to drive me over to Greenwich tomorrow before eight to deliver them."

"I wasn't aware that delivery man was part of my job

description," her father teased. "But I will gladly help out. I had a paper route when I was a kid. Used to get up at the crack of dawn—"

"Thanks." Kylie cut him off before he launched into a long story about his childhood days in Buffalo, New York. She knew the story by heart: the freezing cold winters, biking uphill in three feet of snow, the blinding blizzards. Yet he always delivered the *Sunday News,* no matter the storm conditions. She hoped he would spare her friends the icy details.

"Did I ever tell you about the time it was 10 below?" he began. Kylie rolled her eyes. "Another time, Dad, please. We're exhausted. I think this cupcake order was more than we all bargained for."

"I am so tired," said Lexi. "I can't even feel my fingers anymore from rolling out all that fondant."

"Hey, I'm the one who cracked sixty eggs," said Sadie.

"Jenna dipped all those cupcakes in chocolate ganache, and you don't hear her moaning and groaning."

"That's because she's snoring," giggled Sadie. "She fell asleep!" She gave Jenna a sharp elbow to the ribs. "Wake up, sleepyhead. We've got 250 cupcakes to box!"

Jenna groaned. Her face, covered in flour, was flat on

the kitchen table, and she was drooling. "Five more minutes, Mommy. Please, let me sleep five more minutes!"

Kylie opened a bottle of vanilla extract and waved it under Jenna's nose. Her eyes flew open at the sweet aroma. "What did I miss?" she asked, yawning. "Are we finished? Are we late?"

"We're perfect," Kylie answered. "We just have to pack up and clean the kitchen before my mom freaks out any more than she already has."

It took them another hour to pack all the cupcakes and another to wash all the dishes and bowls and wipe down the kitchen. At 2 a.m. they all passed out on the floor of the living room without even bothering to change into their pj's or roll out their sleeping bags.

When Kylie woke up, the sun was peeking through the curtains and Jenna was snoring in her ear. She rubbed her eyes and felt something sticky on her cheek—it was chocolate ganache. She looked down at her clothes and saw she was still in her apron, and her jeans were covered in splotches of chocolate and batter. "Ugh," she moaned. "What a mess!" Then she glanced over at the clock resting on the mantel.

"7:10!" Kylie jumped to her feet and shook Sadie.

"Wake up! Wake up!" she screamed. "We overslept! We have to get the cupcakes to Greenwich now!"

All the girls stumbled to their feet.

"You're kidding me!" Jenna gasped. "How did this happen?"

"I guess we were so exhausted," Lexi said, "that we forgot to set an alarm."

"Take it easy, girls," Kylie's dad said. He was already dressed in his suit and tie, and dangling his car keys in his hand. "I'm ready to go when you are."

"Now!" shrieked Kylie. "We have to go now or we'll never make it on time."

"Are you sure you don't want to change first?" her dad chuckled.

"No time!" Kylie said, pushing him toward the door. With all the boxes, the car had only enough room for her and her dad in the front seats.

"Break a leg…or an egg…or something," said Jenna, as she waved them off. "I'm not sure how you say good luck for a cupcake delivery!"

☆ ☮ ☆

On the way to the Golden Spoon in Greenwich, Kylie was convinced her father hit every bump in the road, jostling the cupcake boxes stacked on the backseat and in the trunk of their small Corolla.

"Dad, please take it easy," she said, nibbling her nails. "You're killing the cupcakes!"

"If I go any slower, we'll never get there by eight," her father replied. "Your choice."

"Okay, go. Just be *gentle*."

When they arrived, Mr. Ludwig looked as nervous as Kylie. He was pacing the aisles of his gourmet shop, right between the shelves of coffee beans and the boxes of tea biscuits.

"Do you see the time? It is 8:05," he informed them. "My customers come on their way to work. I said I needed these cupcakes by eight."

"Does five minutes really make a difference?" Kylie's dad asked.

"In the bakery business, five minutes makes a great deal of difference," Mr. Ludwig replied. "Would you leave your cupcakes in the oven five minutes longer?"

"No, you're right. I'm so sorry," said Kylie. "We were trying to drive slowly so we didn't mush the cupcakes."

Mr. Ludwig grimaced. "Let me see! Let me see!" he said, grabbing a box from Kylie. When he opened it, one of the cupcakes was dented, its Earth decoration stuck to the inside of the lid.

"This one is unacceptable!" he said, mopping his brow.

"It's just one cupcake—and we made ten extras," Kylie said quickly. "Just in case." Mr. Ludwig opened each box to inspect them. Thankfully, the rest were just fine. His face lit up.

"I am very, very pleased," he told Kylie. "These will be my weekly 'In the Spotlight' gourmet special. I'm sure they'll sell very well, and I will be reordering for next Monday." He handed Kylie a check.

"Next Monday? You mean you want us to do this again?" Kylie couldn't believe it. "I can't! We can't!"

Mr. Ludwig ushered her and her father out the door. "Lovely, thank you for coming," he said, ignoring Kylie's hysteria. "I'll be ringing you soon."

Kylie was in shock all the way back to New Fairfield.

"Well, you wanted to have a successful baking club, and now you do," her dad said, trying to soothe her. "It's great, honey. You should be happy."

Kylie shook her head. "I'm exhausted. I'm sticky. I'm *not* happy."

"You and the girls are just going to have to figure out a

way to make this cupcake thing work for you…or hang up your aprons," her dad said.

Kylie thought about how Juliette had once called her a quitter—when she said she couldn't find any members for the club. Now she had a club, a great one. How could she give it up when things were just starting to take off?

When Kylie got to school, she thought everyone was looking at her funny in the halls. Her hair was a tangled mess, her clothes were covered in stains, and she was sure she smelled like a combination of vanilla and hours-old milk. She truly looked—and felt—like she'd been through a war. How could she possibly do this all over again *and* be a normal fourth grader?

She was in the bathroom, trying to clean herself up, when Meredith breezed in with Emily.

"Eww…if it isn't the Creature from the Black Lagoon," she giggled. "Or is the Swamp Thing? I can't tell."

Kylie thought of what Jenna would do in this situation. She ignored Meredith and continued scrubbing the chocolate off her face and hands.

"What happened to you?" Emily asked.

"I was up all night baking cupcakes for an order," Kylie replied.

"Really?" Emily seemed impressed. "Like you have your own cupcake business?"

Kylie dug into her backpack and pulled out one of the business cards Lexi had made on her computer.

"Cool!" said Emily. "Peace, Love, and Cupcakes."

"More like Freaks, Barf, and Cupcakes," Meredith snickered. She grabbed the card out of Emily's hand and tossed it into the toilet.

"Don't forget to flush." She smiled and walked out.

Kylie may have doubted herself before, but she knew then that there could be no turning back. She had to make PLC work. She had to prove to Meredith that she wasn't a freak or a joke. She had to have the last laugh.

During first period, Lexi passed Kylie a note. "How'd it go?" it read.

Kylie gave her a thumbs-up and went back to doing her social studies before Ms. Shottlan noticed them.

Kylie caught up with her club over lunch. "You want the good news or the bad news?" she asked.

"Good news," said Jenna.

"Mr. Ludwig loved our cupcakes," said Kylie.

"So what could be the bad news?" asked Lexi. "You said he was happy with them."

"Oh, he was happy. The bad news is he said he'd be calling us later this week to place another order of twenty dozen for next Monday."

Both girls were silent. "Yeah, that's what I thought too," said Kylie. "It's just too much for us to handle."

"That wasn't what I was thinking at all," said Lexi. "I was thinking we should make Mr. Ludwig some custom cupcakes just for his shop—maybe with a fondant golden spoon on top. That way the decoration would be one color and take a lot less time."

"And now that I know what chocolate we like, we don't need to bake any samples first," said Jenna. "Kylie, this is totally doable. And it's a lot of money every week."

Just then Sadie raced in. "You wouldn't believe it if I told you," she said breathlessly. "A fifth grader just came up to me in the hall and asked if she could hire us to bake cupcakes for her birthday party this weekend. She loved them at the Eco Fair!"

Kylie pretended to bang her head on the table. This was getting ridiculous. They were not professional bakers— they were just fourth graders with an after-school club! Who were they kidding?

"Wait, Kylie. Before you say no, let me tell you the

theme of the party," begged Sadie. "This girl wants us to make *Twilight* cupcakes."

Kylie's ears perked up. "You mean vampire and were-wolf cupcakes?"

"Just think, Kylie, we could fill them with raspberry puree that squirts out like blood when you take a bite," Jenna suggested.

"And I could make fondant fangs and bats," added Lexi. "Really authentic-looking ones."

Kylie mulled it over. Monster cupcakes were impossible for her to turn down. "You guys come over Friday night, and we can watch a double feature of *New Moon* and *Eclipse* for inspiration," she said. "Maybe try splattering some raspberry puree to see if it looks bloody enough?"

"And what if Mr. Ludwig wants to reorder?" asked Lexi.

"Then we're going to have to charge him 25 cents more a cupcake for Lexi's original golden-spoon design," Kylie said. She was surprised at how much the girls' confidence had lifted her mood. Even though she could barely keep her eyes open, she was actually getting excited to start baking again. Especially the oozing blood cupcakes.

"Oh, and one more thing…" Sadie hesitated. "The girl kind of wants one hundred cupcakes for her party on Sunday."

Lexi gasped, but Kylie reassured her. "Piece of cake," she said with a wink. "We can do it with our eyes closed."

Which was a good thing…because she really, truly needed a nap!

☆ ☮ ☆

After two months of catering cupcakes for birthday parties and the Golden Spoon, PLC had found its groove. Of course, there had been mistakes along the way. Like the time Ms. Fine asked them to make zucchini cupcakes for her dinner party using zucchinis from her garden. They accidentally confused the zucchini with cucumbers (they're both green, after all!) and the cupcakes tasted awful ("Like my mom's face mask!" Jenna said, gagging)— even with mounds of cream-cheese frosting on top. Luckily, they convinced Ms. Fine that carrot cupcakes would be just as yummy—and Sadie's mom had a bunch in their fridge.

Then there was the zoo birthday party for a five-year-old boy who wanted cupcakes that his favorite animal, an elephant, would eat. Kylie did some research: elephants are herbivores and eat cabbage, lettuce, apples, and bananas. So they combined everything into one batter. Kylie looked inside the mixing bowl. The batter was gray, the color of an elephant.

"Eww," said Lexi. "That does not look good."

Jenna stuck one finger in the batter and took a lick. "It tastes even worse than it looks." After five batches of trial and error, they decided on an apple-cinnamon cupcake with banana buttercream frosting. Lexi sculpted cabbage and lettuce leaves out of fondant on top in pretty shades of green.

Jenna took a bite. "Way better!" she pronounced.

The club met on Wednesdays to brainstorm ideas and baked on Fridays for weekend deliveries and on Sundays for the Golden Spoon. Both of Sadie's brothers had even volunteered to help them make the deliveries.

With every batch, the girls got quicker and better. Now even Jenna could crack an egg without getting any shell in the batter. They saved some of their profits to buy a large commercial mixer that could whip up larger batches and assorted piping tips so Lexi could do more designs. Soon they had perfected ten different flavors of cupcakes— including some really creative ones like Peachy Keen, Sour Patch Kid, and Fudge Mud.

☆ ☮ ☆

One afternoon Kylie was in the kitchen, her head buried in cookbooks, looking for a great recipe for a Nutcracker-themed holiday party, when her mother walked in.

"What exactly is a sugarplum?" Kylie asked. "I know they can be fairies and you dream about them at Christmas."

"They're candy," her mom said.

"Perfect! Now we just need to get enough for three dozen cupcakes."

"Well, while you're shopping for ingredients, a lady in the supermarket asked me to give you her number. She's a Blakely parent and she's having a dinner party. Wants you to bake her dessert. I told her no promises, but I would ask the club president."

Kylie nodded, clipping the slip of paper to her PLC notebook. "I'll call her later to get the order."

"Kylie, Dad and I are getting a little concerned. You're spending an awful lot of time with this club. What about your homework?"

"I did all my homework," Kylie replied. Well, almost all. She hadn't read the chapter in her science textbook or started her report on colonial times that was due the next week. But she'd get to it.

"The club is great, and we're really proud of you," her

mom continued. "But we don't want your schoolwork to suffer because of a hobby."

"A hobby?" Kylie cried. "Mom, it's not a hobby! PLC is really important to me and my friends."

"I know it is, but you're only two years away from middle school."

"I practice math all the time when I figure out how much money we have in our budget, or how many minutes we'll need to bake ten dozen cupcakes. And last week I had to research all the planets and constellations for a planetarium birthday party. I'm learning so much, Mom!" Kylie pleaded.

"Okay, you made your point—I know who to call if I want to find the Big Dipper. Just keep it in mind, okay, Kylie? A cupcake business is a lot of responsibility for a grown-up, much less a kid."

Kylie nodded and went back to her recipes. Her mom was right—PLC was growing faster than any of them could have imagined. She tallied up all the orders in her notebook: over the next two months, they would need to bake hundreds and hundreds of cupcakes. Almost every day they got another call or email.

She called an emergency meeting at her house. "I was

looking at our orders, and especially with the holidays coming up, it's a lot," Kylie began.

"How many is a lot?" asked Sadie.

"Well, to be exact, we have orders for 2,440 cupcakes."

Jenna's mouth fell open. "Seriously? In the next eight weeks you want us to bake 2,440 cupcakes?"

"Actually, about 2,500—we should throw in a few extras just in case," Kylie tried to joke.

"It's *nuts*!" cried Jenna. "I have a huge math test coming up and my science project."

Lexi nodded. "Kylie, Jenna's right. We have to turn down some of the orders."

Only a short while ago, her friends had convinced her that PLC could do anything. When she wanted to throw in the towel after that first Golden Spoon delivery, they pushed her onward and upward. Now it was time for her to be the leader and cheer them on. Besides, Kylie couldn't imagine a week without the club baking together.

Part of the excitement was dreaming up the cupcake recipes and designs, but the other part was racing to meet the deadlines. She felt a thrill every time they completed a tower of cupcakes with beautiful swirls of frosting and decorations. Each was a mini masterpiece that every member of PLC had put her heart and soul into.

"I know it's doable if we work together," Kylie insisted. "Let's take a vote. All in favor of keeping the current schedule, raise your hand."

Jenna, Lexi, and Sadie all sat motionless while Kylie's hand waved in the air. "Come on, guys. What happened to making lots of money? Being popular? Having the best club at Blakely?"

"It's a nice idea, Kylie, but I think we bit off more cupcake than we can chew," said Sadie. "And you know there'll be more orders. What then?"

"We take it one day at a time, one order at a time," Kylie replied. "And we'll save some money and get more equipment, the kind they have in real bakeries."

"But we're *not* a real bakery," said Jenna.

"But maybe one day we could be!" Kylie pleaded. "We're real *bakers*."

Lexi considered. "It would be kind of neat to have a store with a big purple awning and cupcakes and peace signs painted all over the walls."

"It isn't such a crazy idea," Kylie said. "Just look at how far we've come in such a short time. Only a few months

Sheryl Berk and Carrie Berk

ago we couldn't even mix up a batch of muffins. And now everyone wants to hire us to bake them cupcakes."

"My mom said I have to pass all my tests," said Sadie. "I can't fall behind. If I do, I have to quit the club and the basketball team."

"We'll help you," promised Kylie. "I'm really good at math, and Lexi is a whiz at English."

"And my family speaks Spanish," said Jenna. "So I can help you with Ms. Rivero's class."

"We can all help each other," said Kylie. "We need each other. I can't do this by myself, guys. Do you think one person could take down Godzilla? No way!"

"I saw that movie," said Sadie. "It took an army to wipe out that big fire-breathing dino. Not a couple of fourth-grade girls."

Jenna giggled. "I bet Mr. Ludwig would turn into Godzilla if we told him no more cupcakes for the Golden Spoon."

Kylie tried again. "All in favor?"

Jenna's hand shot up, then Lexi's, and finally Sadie wiggled her fingers in the air.

"It's unanimous!" Kylie grinned. "Peace, Love, and Cupcakes is still in business!"

120

✫ ☮ ✫

To keep up with all the demand, Juliette suggested the girls meet frequently to brainstorm flavors—especially around the holidays when everyone wanted festive cupcakes. If they planned a few months in advance, they wouldn't be crunched.

"I had this great idea for an Easter flavor," said Jenna. "I call it the Rascally Rabbit!"

Kylie looked confused. "You want to make a Bugs Bunny cupcake?"

"No, an orange carrot cupcake with jelly beans hidden inside. I thought it would be great for Easter."

"Maybe we should call it the 14 Carrot Cupcake and put fourteen carrots in the batter," suggested Sadie.

"We could even top it with edible gold," said Lexi.

"That's so cool!" exclaimed Kylie.

Jenna shot them all a look. "Well, my cupcake name is more fun."

"What else do you think of when you think of Easter?" asked Juliette.

"Chocolate bunnies," said Lexi. "We could do a chocolate cupcake filled with Marshmallow Fluff and topped with a mini chocolate bunny. Maybe call it Somebunny Loves You?"

"Cute!" said Kylie. "And how about doing something with Peeps—you know those cute little marshmallow bunnies and chicks?"

"We could call the cupcake the Peepin' Tom," teased Jenna. "Or the V.I. Peeps! Can I come up with 'em, or can I come up with 'em?"

"I think everyone has some great ideas," said Juliette. "You should figure out a few new flavors every month. Keep things fresh and exciting. Then try them out and perfect them so you're set to go."

Kylie carefully jotted down every cupcake suggestion in her club notebook. She flipped through the pages—she had filled up almost half the book with notes and sketches.

"We've really created some amazing cupcakes," she said. "Remember the Potter PBJ Cupcake we came up with for that Harry Potter–themed Sweet Sixteen?"

"I made all those yellow fondant lightning bolts," said Lexi. "That was really cool."

"What about the baby shower we did for my cousin Brooke?" asked Sadie. "With those cute little rubber duckies on top? And the blue buttercream frosting?"

"My hands hurt from piping all of those—but they were delicious," sighed Jenna. "French vanilla cake. Yum."

"It's really amazing if you think about it," said Juliette. "You guys started out as a school baking club, and you've created a booming business. Just the four of you! You should really be proud of yourselves."

Kylie was proud of PLC—especially of the fact that each of the girls seemed to be growing along with the business. Sadie no longer was embarrassed if she needed extra time or help reading a recipe, and Lexi wasn't afraid anymore to speak up and give her opinions. Then there was Jenna, who had the biggest heart under that tough-girl act and was finally starting to let it show.

When Lexi burst into tears over a fondant rose she couldn't quite get right, Jenna put an arm around her shoulder. "It's way better than any of us could ever do," she told Lexi. "I think it's beautiful—or as my mother would say, '*Que bonita!*'" Jenna's imitation of her mom made Lexi laugh—and she went back to work creating perfect pink roses for a tea-party order.

As for Kylie, she was so busy with PLC that she barely had time to worry about Meredith. When Meredith whispered to Emily in class, "Ewww…what is the Freak wearing today?" Kylie turned around and stared at her stone-faced and unblinking, just as Jenna had taught her. Meredith froze. She actually looked shocked! Take that! Kylie thought.

But Meredith wasn't the slightest bit scared off—she was just plotting her next move. Two days later, Ms. Shottlan announced that the class would be doing "Secret Santa" gifts for the holidays. No one knew who his or her Secret Santa was. That is, until Meredith chose a name out of the hat and blurted it out.

"*OMG!* I got Kylie Carson! I will give someone a hundred Silly Bandz if they will trade with me!" she shrieked.

Kylie was humiliated. She closed her eyes, wishing she could just disappear, like the Invisible Man in one of her favorite monster flicks.

"I'll take Kylie," a voice said. Kylie opened one eye. It was Jack, the farmer who had dropped her in the dirt in the Wellness Day play. And now he wanted to be her Secret Santa! Kylie blushed.

"I mean, she bakes those awesome cupcakes—and maybe she'll make me some if I'm her Secret Santa. I'll trade you, Meredith! And I'll throw in three baseball cards."

"No, I want Kylie!" said Emily. "I'll give you a blueberry Smencil!"

"No fair, I had my hand up first," said Bella. But all she had to offer was a chewed piece of bubble gum.

Kylie was stunned. Speechless. But not as stunned as

Meredith. She flung the slip of paper with Kylie's name on the floor, and Emily, Jack, and Bella all scrambled to retrieve it. Meredith stormed out of the classroom.

Amazingly, cupcakes had done just what Juliette said: they'd made people like Kylie. And for once, they'd put Meredith Mitchell in her place.

12

Deck the Halls... with Cupcakes

The winter dance was always the highlight of fourth grade. The entire gym was transformed into a magical winter wonderland, decorated with twinkly lights, fake snow, and giant snowflakes. This year Kylie had volunteered Peace, Love, and Cupcakes to make one hundred snowman cupcakes.

On top of the white-chocolate buttercream frosting, Lexi had used fondant to create the snowman's "coal" eyes and "carrot" nose, and wrapped each cupcake in a red licorice scarf. They had so much fun baking them. As they piped the frosting, they sang, "Deck the school with tons of cupcakes!"

It was also the first time that the girls had hung outside the kitchen or the school. Kylie had suggested that they go Christmas shopping together to get a present for Juliette, and Kylie's mom was happy to drive the girls to the mall.

"What should we get her?" Sadie asked, looking in the drama section of the bookstore. "Maybe a Shakespeare play? Or how about a book about Canada, where she's from?"

"I think we should get her something from a cooking store," said Jenna. "After all, she's our baking adviser. Like a cool whisk or rolling pin or something."

Kylie thought the gift should be edible. "What about some yummy champagne chocolate truffles—or maple syrup?" she suggested.

But Lexi spotted the perfect gift in the window of a Christmas shop. It was a cupcake ornament made of swirls of different colored glass. It was hand blown and, like a prism, cast a rainbow whenever it caught the light. Even more important, it was one of a kind, just like each girl in PLC.

"Bingo!" said Kylie, gazing in the window. "That's really special and beautiful. And Juliette can hang it on her Christmas tree and think of us."

☆ ☮ ☆

They gave the ornament to Juliette on the night of the dance with a poem that Kylie had written:

Yummy cupcakes are what we make,
Thanks to you, who taught us to bake.
Now we're a team and good friends too.
Juliette, we're so lucky to have you!

As Juliette read the poem, her eyes filled with tears. Kylie was shocked. Her teacher didn't seem the crying type. Kylie hoped the ornament was okay…maybe Juliette had one already? Maybe she didn't like celebrating Christmas or have a tree?

"Um, we hope you like it," Kylie said softly.

"I love it," Juliette replied. "This was so thoughtful, girls. It's lovely. This year I was new at Blakely, just like you once were, Kylie. I wasn't sure if people would like me. But this club and all of you made me feel very appreciated." They all hugged before making their way in to the party.

Everyone was swarming around the dessert table and PLC's scrumptious cupcakes.

"Delicious, ladies," said Ms. Shottlan. "I especially love the chocolate that oozes out when you take a bite."

"That was my idea," bragged Jenna. "I call it the Chocolate Avalanche."

"Well, it's yummy," Ms. Bayder broke in. "And very artistic."

"Thanks," Lexi said. That was the first time she had accepted a compliment—and the credit—for something she had done. She hadn't even blushed. Kylie was proud of her.

It was Kylie's first time for something as well. She had never attended a school dance before—and she was having a blast. She'd even bought a new outfit for the occasion: a cherry red sweater with white snowflakes and a black ruffled skirt.

"You look nice," said Emily. "I think you guys are such good bakers that you should be on the *Martha Stewart Show* or something."

"We're so busy that we wouldn't have time!" replied Kylie. "But thanks."

"I bet you're making lots and lots of money," said Jeremy. "Maybe you need an accountant—I'm available, you know. I got a 99 on the last math test."

"We're doing just fine, but thanks for the offer," Kylie said, chuckling. "My dad's an accountant. And, no, we're not rich. Ingredients, mixers, and pans are really expensive."

Everyone, it seemed, wanted to talk to the girls about cupcakes.

"I feel like an MVP," said Sadie. "Jack Yu offered to do

my homework for two nights if I'd give his mom the recipe for our Chocolate Avalanche filling!"

Jenna shook her head. "That's my secret, and I will never tell," she said. "Not even if you torture me."

They were all dancing to "Jingle Bell Rock" when Meredith seized the microphone to make an announcement.

"Can I have your attention, please?" she called.

"Oh, look—it's the Ice Queen," whispered Jenna. Kylie thought Meredith certainly did look the part. Her entire dress was covered in long, dangling crystals that sparkled like icicles under the gym's lights.

"As president of the student council, I just want to give a shout-out to all the kids who helped with the dance this year: Emily for helping me make and hang the decorations, Abby and Bella for putting up all the posters…"

Kylie waited patiently for Meredith to say thanks to Peace, Love, and Cupcakes. After all, they had made all these cupcakes for free, and they were the hit of the party.

"Oh, yes, and a special shout-out to Kylie Carson. This one's for you!" She cued the DJ, who began playing "The Monster Mash" over the loudspeakers.

The gym erupted in laughter. "She did *not* just do that!" Sadie sighed.

"Oh yes, she did," said Kylie, who tried her hardest to smile and pretend it didn't bother her while everyone pointed to her and made silly monster faces.

As if that wasn't enough, Meredith had another trick up her sequined sleeve.

"Eww!" shrieked Abby, suddenly throwing one of the snowman cupcakes to the floor. "There's a bug in this cupcake!"

"Mine too!" screamed Bella.

Suddenly, everyone at the dance was tossing their cupcakes in the trash.

"Wait! Wait!" cried Kylie. "There are no bugs in these cupcakes!"

Abby held out her hand. "Really? Then what's this?"

Jenna took what looked like a red spider from her palm. She sniffed and took a bite.

"*Ick!* She eats bugs!" squealed Abby.

"Pul-lease," groaned Jenna. "This is a *gummy* spider. Totally edible. Cherry, I believe."

"Well, mine is a black beetle!" said Bella, pointing to the bug she had flung to the floor.

Jenna inspected it. "Black licorice," she said.

"Someone told those two to say there were bugs in their cupcakes," Kylie fumed. "Do you want to guess who?"

"And now everyone is totally grossed out and won't touch them," said Lexi. "This is terrible."

"This is Meredith," sighed Kylie.

Just then, Meredith appeared back at the microphone.

"Everyone, not to worry! My mom and I have baked delicious peppermint brownies for the entire party. Dig in!" Platters of fudge brownies dotted with chunks of candy cane suddenly appeared.

Jenna took a bite. "No way she made these," she said. "They're way too professional. I'll bet you Meredith bought them at the Golden Spoon."

"It doesn't matter," said Kylie. "Now everyone thinks she's a great baker—and we're losers."

"Wow, can you give me the recipe for these?" begged Emily. Meredith grinned. "Sure! I can even make you some and bring them to school next week."

"That is so nice of you!" replied Emily. "You should start a brownie business." Meredith shot Kylie a devious look. "Who knows? Maybe I will. I could call it Peace, Love, and *Brownies*!"

Kylie gasped. "Don't, Kylie," Jenna said, putting a hand on her shoulder. "She wants you to freak out. Don't let her get to you."

Kylie felt the tears stinging in the corners of her eyes—but she didn't cry. She didn't tell Meredith what she really felt like screaming: "You ruin everything, and I hate your guts!" She just stood there, numb.

"We'll think of something," Sadie assured her. "Don't worry, Kylie. We won't let her get away with this."

Kylie wasn't listening. Everything was a blur of lights and voices and shiny snowflakes. "I need to get out of here," she said. "I'm sorry."

She pushed past the crowd and headed for the gym door. When she glanced back, Meredith was once again the center of attention, and PLC had been quickly forgotten. Her three friends looked sad and defeated. But Kylie was too upset herself to try to raise their spirits. She couldn't lead them at this moment. Between the Monster Mash song, the sabotaged cupcakes, and Meredith's announcement about starting a brownie business, Kylie felt like she had been buried by an avalanche.

13

The End of PLC?

Kylie just couldn't shake the memory of the winter dance disaster. Two days later her mom noticed her moping around the house and commented, "You don't seem like yourself, honey." It was Sunday taco night, and Kylie hadn't even touched a bite of her favorite refried beans.

"I'm fine," she shrugged.

"Did something happen at school?" her father asked.

Kylie shrugged again.

"Everything okay with your club?" her mom tried.

Another shrug.

Her parents looked at each other, puzzled. "We can't help you unless you tell us what's wrong," said her mom.

"I'm brilliant—but I'm not psychic," teased her dad.

"I have homework," Kylie said, pushing her plate away. "May I be excused?" Her mom nodded.

Kylie flopped on her bed and hugged her giant panda

bear, Koko. Her dad had won him for her at the Jupiter Fireman's Carnival when she was three years old, and she just couldn't get rid of the bear, even though he had one eye and his arms and legs were all floppy and missing most of their stuffing. Koko always had a knack for making her feel better. Yet this time that didn't seem to be working.

Nothing Meredith had done to her in the past had been half as bad as this. Kylie could stand the name-calling and the mean pranks. But threatening to steal her club's name and business right out from under her? That was too, too much. Meredith was hurting more than just Kylie—she was hurting Kylie's friends and Juliette as well. That club meant everything to them, and they had all grown so much from being a part of it.

Mostly they had grown closer together. They were a rock-solid team, there for each other when things got tough. And Kylie couldn't stand to see Meredith destroy that! She didn't know what to do, or if she had the strength to do it. But she had to do something. Not just for her, but for Lexi, Sadie, and Jenna. And for what PLC stood for.

There was a knock on the door and her mom peeked into her room. "Kylie, you have company."

When she came out to the living room, there were Sadie, Lexi, and Jenna.

"We thought maybe you could use some cheering up," said Lexi, handing Kylie a wrapped box. It was if they had read her mind.

"What is it?" Kylie asked.

"We made you brownies filled with gummy worms," joked Jenna. "Kidding!"

"Go ahead and open it," said Lexi, anxiously.

Kylie tore away the ribbon and wrapping paper and opened the box. Inside was a T-shirt with the Peace, Love, and Cupcakes logo on it. "It's awesome," she said. "I love it."

"I had them made as Christmas gifts for all of us," Lexi explained. "But I thought maybe you could use it a few weeks early."

"I'm not sure we'll be needing shirts if we don't have a club or a business anymore," Kylie sighed.

Sadie pulled a piece of paper out of her jacket pocket. "Oh, trust me—we have a business! We have two new orders for holiday parties and three more for New Year's Eve!"

"Really?" said Kylie. "You mean Meredith's buggy cupcakes didn't ruin it?"

"We should actually thank her," said Jenna. "After you

left, Jack started daring all the boys to eat them. There wasn't a single one left."

"But what about Peace, Love, and Brownies?" asked Kylie.

"I heard Meredith tell Emily she was way too busy with her other activities," said Sadie. "She's competing in some big gymnastics tournament in January and practicing every day. She just said it to make you mad."

"Forget about that. We can't bake without our cupcake club president," added Lexi.

"Yeah," Sadie chimed in. "We had to make a dozen Blueberry Cobbler Cupcakes today, and Jenna thought it was blackberry."

"*You* got your berries mixed up?" Kylie couldn't believe it. Jenna never messed up an ingredient.

Jenna dug her hands in her pockets and tried to pretend it was no biggie. "Well, it happens," she said quietly. "I read the order wrong. You have terrible handwriting, Sadie!"

Sadie chuckled. "Anyway, enough moping. We need you. Especially if Meredith goes all Godzilla on us again. We can't fight her without you."

"I guess if you put it that way…how could I turn down a good monster battle?" Kylie said, slipping the T-shirt over her head.

"Hey, I just thought of something," Jenna said, getting that glint in her eye. "We're like Dracula. We take a staking...but keep on baking!"

The girls all groaned and laughed—and went into the kitchen to start planning their next order schedule.

14

No Business Like Cupcake Business

The girls were hard at work at Kylie's house, whipping up one hundred cupcakes for a rock 'n' roll–themed Sweet Sixteen party when the phone rang. No one had a spare hand to get it.

"Mom, can you grab that?" called Kylie from the kitchen. "My hands are full of mocha caramel batter!"

Her mom could barely say "Hello" before a woman interrupted.

"Is this Peace, Love, and Cupcakes?" the woman demanded.

"Uh, sort of, yes…that's my daughter's business," said her mom.

"I need to place an order. A big order. An important order," the woman bellowed. "Right away!"

"Kylie," her mom called. "There is a lady who would like to place an order—and she's a little impatient."

"Put it on speaker!" Kylie replied. Her mom walked into the kitchen with the phone, and the woman's voice suddenly boomed through the house: "This is Eloise Mitchell. I am throwing a tenth birthday party for my daughter, Meredith, two weeks from Sunday. I tried one of your cupcakes at the Golden Spoon and it was delicious. Mr. Ludwig says you're the best—and nothing but the best will do for my daughter."

Kylie's face went pale. "*No way!*" she mouthed to her fellow club members. Meredith! Of all people!

"Is anyone there?" Mrs. Mitchell huffed.

"Yes, we're here," said Jenna. "Can you hang on a sec?" She placed the phone call on mute so they could discuss the situation.

"I am no-way, no-how going to bake cupcakes for Meredith Mitchell!" Kylie screamed. "N-O!" She made a gagging face.

Her mom raised an eyebrow. "Kylie, why would you say that?"

"Because Meredith Mitchell is evil. She's the meanest girl in school!" Kylie insisted. It had been two months since the winter dance, but Kylie had not forgotten what Meredith had done. She would *never* forget.

"That may be so, but business is business," her mother

explained. "You shouldn't let your personal opinions cloud your decisions. Sometimes I don't love all the freelance stories my editor gives me to write for *Nature Magazine*—some are very hard, and some are very boring. I had to write one about the flat-tailed horned lizard yesterday."

"Your mom is right," Jenna said. "I think we should at least hear what Mrs. Mitchell wants PLC to do. At least it won't involve lizards. Yuck!"

"I don't care," Kylie replied. "I refuse to take this order. Besides, we have a million Valentine's Day cupcakes to make and deliver."

"You're not the only member of the club, remember?" said Sadie. "We all get a vote, Kylie. That's what you always tell us."

Ugh. Sadie was right. That was exactly what Kylie told her friends when they disagreed on a cupcake flavor or decoration—or when she asked them to do another two dozen cupcakes for a last-minute birthday party. Everyone's vote counted when it came to the club. So Kylie pressed the mute button again. "Go ahead, Mrs. Mitchell," she said through gritted teeth.

"The birthday party will have an Italian theme, because that is Meredith's tenth birthday present. We are taking her to Rome this summer," she continued. "Doesn't that sound simply *mah*-voo-lous?"

"*Mah*-voo-lous!" Jenna giggled, imitating Mrs. Mitchell. "She's one lucky girl." Kylie shot her a look.

"I want you to make a Leaning Tower of Pisa out of five hundred cupcakes. And I want the cupcakes to be filled with cannoli cream."

"That's a really tall order—literally," said Jenna. "This would have to be a huge cupcake tower!"

"Yes, I want it five feet tall with an Italian flag on top," said Mrs. Mitchell.

Kylie gasped. This order was getting crazier by the minute! "We've never done anything like that."

"I will pay you $1,500 if you do an outstanding job," Meredith's mother promised. Now it was Jenna, Sadie, and Lexi's turn to gasp. Sadie hit the mute button so they could confer one more time.

"You know, $1,500 is a ton of money!" Sadie said. "Kylie, I really want to get a new bike this summer. This would definitely pay for it!"

"I don't think you could pay me a million dollars to bake for Meredith," Kylie protested. "Let her go somewhere else for her cupcakes."

"But it's such a great project for us," Lexi pushed. She had already begun to sketch a tower of cupcakes with Roman columns in between the tiers. "It would be amazing."

"I say we should do it," Sadie piped up.

"Me too," said Jenna.

Kylie sighed. She was outvoted. But it simply burned her to do anything nice for Meredith. After all the horrible, evil, demonic things she had done to ruin Kylie's life. She made Dracula look like an amateur! And now Kylie was supposed to create a gorgeous cupcake tower for Meredith's birthday party so everyone would ooh and ahh? The idea made her so mad that her head pounded.

"Please!" the girls pleaded. "Please, Kylie?"

She went back to Mrs. Mitchell on the phone. "I guess you have yourself a cupcake Tower of Pisa," she sighed as the girls high-fived in the background.

"Splendid," said Mrs. Mitchell. "Just one condition: you cannot use any cinnamon in the cupcakes. Meredith is allergic to cinnamon."

Lexi wrote down all the details of the order: the date, the time, the number of cupcakes, and in big, red letters: *No Cinnamon!*

Kylie looked at the order form and shook her head. How

had she gotten herself into this? She should have stood her ground. She should have refused. Yes, the club might have been angry with her at first, but the girls knew how much she hated Meredith. They would have forgiven her eventually. But her mom did have a point: this was business, and that meant being professional and putting her feelings aside. And everyone was so excited for the money…it was a *lot* of money.

"Boy, Mrs. Mitchell was really serious about that no-cinnamon part," Sadie said. "Like Meredith's head would explode or something if there was any cinnamon in these cupcakes."

Just then Kylie had an idea. A deliciously dastardly idea. But no one, not even the members of Peace, Love, and Cupcakes, could know about it.

A Pisa Cake

The two weeks before Meredith's tenth birthday party flew by. The girls had needed several days to perfect the cannoli-cream recipe and figure out how to make the Tower of Pisa lean. Lexi had the idea of making large cardboard circles covered with an Italian map to hold the cupcakes and Styrofoam cylinders in between the layers to look like columns. But when they got to the very top…

"It's too straight. The Tower of Pisa is supposed to be crooked," sighed Sadie.

"Well, maybe if I stack the three top layers a little off center," Lexi said. The structure tumbled down around her. "Hmm…well, that didn't work."

It was Sadie's dad, a contractor, who finally came up with a solution. He suggested that the base be slightly wider at the bottom and that they put one long wooden dowel through the cardboard tiers from top to bottom to keep the structure from toppling.

"That should do it," he said. "Just make sure nobody bangs into it while dancing and you'll be fine."

He also pointed out that the Styrofoam columns should be hot-glued into place. Kylie thought that would work well but then shuddered when she remembered how Meredith had hot-glued her turnip green hat at the Wellness Day play.

"You okay?" asked Jenna.

"Yeah, fine." Kylie quickly recovered. "It's just a lot of hard work."

"For someone who doesn't deserve it? I know. I get it, Kylie. There are a lot of people who pick on me in school too. Meredith is not exactly my favorite person either."

Kylie nodded. "Do you ever wish you could get even with those people who call you names, Jenna?" she asked.

"Get even? Sure. But then my mom always tells me, 'Two wrongs don't make a right.' Or 'Why waste all your time and energy on people who just don't matter?'" Jenna took a lick of cannoli-cream filling. "This is the best flavor we have ever made. Seriously, you have to try this!"

Kylie took a taste. "You're right." She meant about the

filling, but she also wondered if Jenna wasn't right about getting even. What would it accomplish? Would it stop Meredith from bullying her? Not likely. Yet for once, just once, she wished Meredith could understand what it felt like to be in her shoes, to be humiliated in front of the whole class or even the entire school. She pictured Meredith's cheeks flushing red and her throwing a wild tantrum while everyone laughed and pointed at her. She would burst into tears and probably throw things. Kylie smiled. Revenge would be so sweet! She could almost taste it.

"Kylie, did you hear what I said?" Sadie tapped her on the shoulder. "You're like on another planet today!"

"Sorry," Kylie replied. "I was just thinking about the party."

"I said we'll have to bring all the cupcakes with us and put the whole thing together at the country club," Sadie said. "Otherwise we'll never fit this all in the back of Sadie's dad's truck."

"Right, we'll assemble it all there and put the finishing touches on the cupcakes," Kylie nodded. Lexi had had the idea of putting a dusting of cocoa powder and crushed ice-cream cones and a sprinkling of mini chocolate chips on top of each cupcake—so it really looked like a cannoli. They would give Meredith a giant-sized version of the cupcake with red, green, and white candles (the colors of the Italian flag) on it to blow out.

"Do you think these candles will be too big?" Lexi asked, holding up the six-inch tapers. "They look so nice!"

"Nah, Meredith has plenty of hot air," Jenna chuckled. "She'll be able to blow them out, *no problema*!"

The morning of the party, Kylie meticulously checked every box of cupcakes before her friends arrived for the delivery. Juliette also came to help them load and set up.

"These are beautiful," she told Kylie. "You guys should be really proud. You've outdone yourselves."

Kylie packed up extra frosting, cocoa powder, and chocolate chips—just in case they needed to do some emergency repairs. "I think we're all set," she said, just as Sadie and her dad were pulling up in front of her house with their truck.

"I'll start taking these out," said Juliette. The giant cupcake for Meredith was sitting in its own box to present to the birthday girl. Kylie opened it and peeked inside. It was a masterpiece. Lexi had created a dramatic flourish of frosting around the edges. She had dotted the top of the cupcake with cocoa powder and chocolate chips and written "Happy

10th Birthday, Meredith" in gold piping gel in the center. Kylie made sure everyone was busy outside loading the truck. Then she reached for a small jar on the spice rack and placed it in her jacket pocket.

"Got the jumbo cupcake?" Sadie called through the front door.

"Coming!" said Kylie, carrying the box outside. "Let's go!"

The country club was decorated to look exactly like a street in Rome. The ballroom was filled with Roman statues and columns with vines climbing to the ceiling. The buffet table was set with every kind of Italian food imaginable: lasagna, spaghetti and meatballs, pepperoni pizza. And in the center of the room was a replica of the Trevi Fountain. As the banquet manager flipped a switch, the fountain suddenly lit up and began to flow.

"Wow!" gushed Jenna. "This is some party!"

"I'll say," said Juliette. "I haven't seen this much Roman scenery since I did *Julius Caesar* on stage!"

"This table in the corner behind the curtain is for you to set up your tower," the manager instructed. "You'd better get to it. Guests arrive in two hours."

The girls worked up to the last minute stacking the cupcakes on each tier. Lexi climbed on a ladder to reach the very top of the tower. She planted an Italian flag in a cup-cake. Then they sat back and watched as Meredith's friends and family all arrived.

"I guess we can go now," Lexi said to the group. "Mission accomplished."

"No!" Kylie piped up. "I mean, we want to make sure everything goes okay, right?"

Sadie looked puzzled. "You want to stay and see Meredith? I thought you hated her."

"I just think she should know who is responsible for this amazing cupcake tower," said Kylie. She just couldn't leave. Not yet.

Juliette nodded. "You should make sure that Mrs. Mitchell is pleased before you guys dash out of here—no matter what you think of Meredith."

"And sample some of the appetizers!" Jenna chimed in. "Did you guys see those mozzarella sticks?"

At exactly 2 o'clock, the lights dimmed and the guest of honor made a grand entrance. A hush fell over the room as Meredith—wearing a red satin party dress and with her hair in an elegant updo—appeared in the doorway with her mother.

"*Surprise!*" the crowd cheered. Meredith waved royally

and gushed, "Oh, I had no idea! I am so surprised! Thank you, thank you all!" Then she beamed at her mom, who was wearing a red satin dress as well—and looked like a grown-up version of Meredith.

"So much for a surprise party—she totally knew," said Sadie. "Can we leave *now*?"

"A few more minutes," Kylie said, hushing her. "I want to see her blow out the candles on her cupcake."

"Okay, now you are acting *really* weird," Jenna whispered. "What's up, Kylie?"

"Nothing," she replied. "Shh! Her mom is making a speech!"

"I would like to wish my beautiful, brilliant daughter Meredith a happy tenth birthday and many more," Mrs. Mitchell began. "I do hope you like your party—and your Leaning Tower of Pisa!" The banquet manager pulled back a red curtain to reveal the cupcake display.

There were murmurs of "Awesome!" "Wow!" and "Incredible!" from the crowd. A waiter came in with the giant cupcake on a silver platter with the candles all lit. "Make a wish, sweetheart!" Meredith's dad told her.

As Meredith took a deep breath to blow out the candles, her face suddenly looked strange. Her cheeks turned bright red, her eyes watered, her lips quivered, her nose twitched.

Here it comes, Kylie thought to herself and crossed her fingers.

Suddenly, Meredith let out a huge sneeze!

"Gesundheit!" said the waiter, ducking under the platter. But he kept holding the cupcake in front of her.

"I…*achoo!*…can't…*achoo!*…stop…*achoo!*…sneezing!" cried Meredith. "Take that…*achoo!*…thing…*achoo!*…away from me…*achoo!*" She pushed the waiter away, and he stumbled against the tower, sending dozens of cupcakes flying in every direction.

"Oh no!" screamed Mrs. Mitchell.

Frosting sprayed everywhere, and as Meredith tried to run away, she slipped on a pile of cannoli cream and slid across the entire ballroom floor. Kylie looked around and saw no one was roaring with laughter. In fact, they looked shocked. Then she saw Meredith sprawled on her back on the floor. She wasn't throwing a tantrum. She wasn't bright red with embarrassment. She was just sneezing her head off! She looked pretty miserable…and scared.

The guests huddled around her, and Mr. and Mrs. Mitchell rushed to her side. "Oh, my poor baby!" Mrs. Mitchell cried.

"Let's get you some fresh air!" They helped Meredith up and out the door of the ballroom. She was still sneezing, and her nose was as red as her party dress.

"Sorry, everyone. We have to get Meredith home and to a doctor. Party's over," said Mr. Mitchell. There were groans of disappointment as the two hundred guests emptied out of the ballroom.

"*OMG*," gasped Jenna.

"What just happened?" Juliette asked.

Sadie, Lexi, and Jenna looked at each other—then at Kylie. They waited for her to say something. But Kylie was speechless. She felt awful, worse than she had ever felt— even after the time Meredith put a Post-it on her back that said "Monster," and she walked around wearing it all day. This wasn't the revenge she had imagined. Yes, the party was ruined and Meredith had left feeling horrible. But Kylie wasn't much in the mood to celebrate. It didn't feel very good.

She looked around the room. Their beautiful Leaning Tower of Pisa had toppled to the floor. Whatever cupcakes had survived the fall had been trampled by the guests leaving. Lexi had tears in her eyes. "All my hard work," she cried. "Ruined."

"And no one will get to taste our delicious cannoli-cream cupcakes," said Jenna.

"What do you think made Meredith sneeze like that?" asked Sadie. "It was freaky!"

Kylie couldn't look any of her PLC club members in the eye. She fingered the spice jar in her pocket and was grateful when the banquet manager chased them out of the ballroom. All the way home in Juliette's car, no one spoke a single word.

All night Kylie tossed and turned in bed. She wondered what had happened to Meredith. What if she was in the hospital? Then she thought about Jenna, Sadie, and Lexi—after all the hard work and long hours they had put in on those cupcakes, she had ruined it. She had let down her friends, and that hurt most of all. She felt like her whole life was coming unraveled—like the wraps unwinding on the Mummy.

When she saw that Meredith wasn't in school on Monday, Kylie feared the worst. *What if she's really sick or dying and it's all my fault?* I could keep quiet and pretend I don't know anything, she reasoned with herself. Then she pictured poor Meredith in a hospital bed, hooked up to wires and tubes as doctors struggled to figure out what was wrong with her.

"If we only knew what caused the allergic reaction, we could save her!" the doctor in her daydream said.

Kylie suddenly recalled the time she had accidentally dropped her mom's diamond engagement ring down the drain and then pretended not to know where it was.

"You're sure you weren't playing with it?" her dad had asked her.

Kylie was five years old and terrified that her parents would punish her.

Then she saw her mom sobbing and frantically turning the house upside down. "Mommy, I dropped it down there," she said, pointing to the bathroom sink. Luckily, the plumber was able to fish it out, and instead of being mad, her mom was relieved and hugged her.

Kylie knew Meredith was not about to thank her or hug her for coming clean. Still…

"If only someone would tell us what caused this," Mrs. Mitchell sobbed in Kylie's fantasy. *"My poor, poor darling daughter…sneezing herself into a coma!"*

Kylie shook the awful picture out of her head—but she knew what she had to do. She called an emergency meeting of Peace, Love, and Cupcakes after school in the drama room.

"I have something I have to tell you guys," she said. Then she took a deep breath. "I put cinnamon on top of Meredith's cupcake."

Juliette shook her head. "Kylie, I am very disappointed in you," she said. "You knew Meredith was allergic."

Kylie braced herself for her friends' reactions.

"I kinda thought you did," said Jenna. "I had a feeling that's what made Meredith sneeze like that."

"Why?" asked Lexi. "We all agreed we'd do the cupcakes for the party. Why did you want to destroy all our hard work? Now no one will ever hire us again—not after Mrs. Mitchell spreads the word."

"I feel awful," said Kylie. She couldn't keep the tears from streaming down her cheeks. "I just was so mad at Meredith."

"What Meredith did to you at the Wellness Day play wasn't nice," Juliette said. "But what you did…it was dangerous. You're lucky all Meredith did was get a whiff of that cinnamon. What if she had eaten it? Who knows what might have happened to her then!"

"It wasn't just the Wellness Day play, Juliette," Sadie said, defending her friend. "Meredith has been bullying Kylie since third grade. And it's really getting bad."

"Is that true?" Juliette asked. Kylie nodded. "Then why didn't you tell someone? Me? Principal Fontina? Your parents?"

Kylie shrugged. "I thought it would make things worse."

"Well, now you've gone ahead and made things worse on your own," Juliette replied. "You need to apologize to Meredith and her parents. You need to tell them what you did. It's the right thing to do."

Kylie shuddered. The thought of facing Meredith was terrifying. She'd be livid when she heard about the cinnamon. This was ten times worse than hitting her in the eye with a sneaker.

"We'll go with you," offered Sadie, putting her arm around her friend.

"No," Kylie responded. "I did this, not you guys. You shouldn't have to take the blame."

"I'll drive you there now," said Juliette.

"Can't it wait?" asked Kylie. "Like maybe till school is out for the summer and I won't have to see Meredith every day?"

Juliette shook her head. "Kylie, you know you have to do this."

In the car ride to Meredith's house, Kylie didn't know

what to say to her club adviser. Juliette had always had so much faith in her—and Kylie had disappointed her terribly.

"I'm sorry," Kylie said.

"I know you are," said Juliette. "But it's not me you should apologize to. I understand why you did it, Kylie, but I'm surprised that someone as smart as you couldn't see right from wrong." Kylie hated when Juliette sounded "teacherly." It made her feel very guilty.

"I just wanted to get even with Meredith," Kylie explained. "I thought it would feel great."

"But it didn't feel great, did it?"

"No, it felt awful."

"Maybe you should think about why Meredith is mean to you," Juliette said.

"Why? Because she hates me!" Kylie cried. "She has always hated me and she always will."

"But *why* does she hate you? Maybe because she sees something in you that scares her, that threatens her."

Kylie thought about it. Could Meredith really be scared of her? It didn't seem possible. Nothing scared Meredith. Then again, she had looked very upset that day when the kids were all fighting to be Kylie's Secret Santa. Meredith was almost in tears.

"Remember when I told you that kids used to make fun of my red hair in school when I was a kid? Well, one kid in particular loved to torture me: Evangelique Girard. Angie for short. She had long, shiny black hair and I was so jealous. But you want to know something funny? Years later, when we were both in college, I bumped into her in a Starbucks. She had dyed her hair bright red—I didn't even recognize her!"

"So Angie was jealous of you?" Kylie asked. "She really liked your red hair?"

"Yup. And her teasing and bullying were how she dealt with those feelings. Just think about it, okay?"

Juliette parked the car in front of the house. "Time to face the music," she said, squeezing Kylie's hand. "Take a deep breath. You'll be fine."

Inside, Kylie was slightly relieved to see that Meredith wasn't in the hospital like she had imagined. She was actually lying on the couch in a fluffy pink robe, covered with a cashmere blanket. Her eyes were all bloodshot and swollen, and her nose was still pink. Mrs. Mitchell hovered over her, plumping her pillows and spoon-feeding her sips of chamomile tea. "It's simply horrible," Meredith's mom told Juliette. "Her throat is still scratchy and sore from all that sneezing."

"The doctor said she'll be just fine," Mr. Mitchell interjected. "Just an allergic reaction to something in the ballroom…probably dust."

"Ahem." Juliette cleared her throat and gave Kylie a little push.

"About that…" Kylie began. She turned to face Meredith, who was already shooting her a nasty look. "Meredith, I owe you an apology. You see, I kind of sprinkled some cinnamon on your birthday cupcake."

"What?" shrieked Mrs. Mitchell. "I specifically told you *not* to use cinnamon!"

"Perhaps it was an accident?" offered Mr. Mitchell. "I'm sure Kylie didn't do this intentionally."

Kylie shook her head. "No, sir. I did. I wanted to get back at Meredith."

Mrs. Mitchell's eyes looked wide and wild. "You did *what*? I am going to call Principal Fontina this instant and have you expelled from Blakely!"

Kylie gulped. "Please! Wait! Let me explain!" She told Meredith's parents about all the things Meredith had done to her: tripping her down the stairs of the bus, calling her names, sabotaging her turnip costume, putting bugs in her snowman cupcakes.

"I just wanted Meredith to see what it felt like to be me," she said.

"I don't believe it," Mrs. Mitchell said, turning to Meredith. "She's just jealous of you, isn't she, darling?"

Meredith nodded and croaked out, "Yes, Mommy."

"I will make sure that everyone in Blakely, everyone in town, knows what you did. Your cupcake business is over. You'll be lucky if I don't call the sheriff himself!"

"You'd better go now, Kylie," Mr. Mitchell said.

Juliette took Kylie by the elbow and pulled her toward the door. "I'm proud of you for doing that, Kylie," she said. "I know it was really hard. Don't worry. I'll talk to Principal Fontina and explain what's been going on. You're not the only one to blame here."

That didn't make Kylie feel much better. She had become what she hated most about Meredith—a mean bully bent on getting even, no matter who she hurt along the way. Peace, Love, and Cupcakes was over—and it was all her fault. She'd gone against everything the club stood for. How could she face Lexi, Jenna, and Sadie again? She deserved whatever punishment Principal Fontina had in store for her. And from the angry, determined look on Mrs. Mitchell's face, it was going to be pretty bad.

Just Desserts

At 10 a.m. sharp Tuesday morning, Kylie was summoned to Principal Fontina's office.

"Good luck," Ms. Shottlan said, giving her a weak smile. Abby and Bella stared and whispered as Kylie got up from her desk and walked toward the door. Did everyone at Blakely know what she had done to Meredith? Were they all rooting for her to be kicked out of school?

She walked down the hallway, her heart pounding in her throat. When she got to the principal's office, she was shocked to find her parents and Mr. Mitchell already there, seated at the desk. Juliette was also there, but she wasn't her usual cheery self. Her face looked sad and uncertain.

"Kylie, please come in," Principal Fontina began. Her voice was stern. "I have explained the situation to your parents, as it has been explained to me by Ms. Dubois and Mr. Mitchell."

Kylie gulped and looked to her mom and dad for support. Her mom bit her lip, and her father tapped his foot on the side of the chair—a habit she'd noticed he only did when he was worried about something. She knew she should have told her parents last night what happened, but she just couldn't. She knew they would be furious at her for doing something so spiteful. Especially her mom, who volunteered all the time at Blakely, the senior citizens' complex, and the library. She'd be crushed that her daughter was so cruel and unfeeling. How would her mother be able to show her face at the next PTA meeting when she had such a horrible kid?

"I will let Mr. Mitchell speak first," Principal Fontina said.

Kylie faced Meredith's father. At that moment, she wished she could turn into a vampire bat and fly out the office window. But no such luck; she had to stand there and take it.

"Kylie, I am very sorry," said Mr. Mitchell. Kylie stared in disbelief. He sounded like he was apologizing.

"What Meredith has been doing to you…well, there is just no excuse for it." Kylie was stunned. Meredith would never confess, so how did Mr. Mitchell know what Meredith had done?

Principal Fontina read her mind. "Your friends Sadie, Lexi, and Jenna filled me in on the bullying, and Ms. Dubois was a witness as well."

Kylie looked at Juliette, who gave her a wink. Her friends had stood by her. None of them had been worried about challenging Meredith or Mrs. Mitchell or what she might do to the club. They were only worried about her, Kylie.

Mr. Mitchell nodded. "Kylie, we are so sorry for our daughter's poor behavior. We understand why you did what you did this weekend. In a way, Meredith finally got her just desserts. And she will be calling you today to apologize."

Kylie let out a huge sigh of relief. "So I am not expelled?"

"No," said Principal Fontina. "But what you did wasn't right either, Kylie. And I cannot just excuse it."

Kylie sighed. Here it comes…

"To make up for what you did to Meredith Mitchell, I want you and the members of Peace, Love, and Cupcakes to bake for school Field Day—enough for all the students and teachers at Blakely. That's seven hundred cupcakes, to be exact."

Kylie laughed. "We can do that…I think!" Then she hugged her parents, Juliette, and Mr. Mitchell.

"Thank you," she told him.

"And you don't have to worry about Meredith making your life miserable anymore," Mr. Mitchell told her. "We've grounded Meredith for the rest of the school year. No more hip-hop, no more TV, no more gymnastics, no more shopping. And if she ever tries anything again…"

"You come directly to me," said Principal Fontina. "No more taking matters into your own hands."

"Okay," said Kylie. "I promise."

As she walked back to her classroom, she felt like a huge dark cloud had just been lifted. She couldn't wait to find Lexi, Sadie, and Jenna and give them each a huge hug. She was so relieved and happy. Maybe now Meredith would finally leave her alone. Even better, PLC wasn't out of business. In fact, things were only just beginning.

Winner Bakes All

"Go, Sadie!" Kylie cheered as her friend leaped over a hurdle and landed in a blow-up kiddie pool filled with whipped cream. Sadie pumped her fist in the air.

"Yes!" she shouted. "I win!" Sadie had already won a gold medal for the potato-sack race, the crazy-shoe relay, and the backward basketball toss. Kylie marveled; even blindfolded and shooting behind her back, Sadie could sink five baskets!

"You rocked it!" Kylie called, giving her the thumbs-up. Field Day at Blakely was all about silly obstacle courses, team spirit, and good sportsmanship. Everyone loved it— especially the teachers who got to invent and referee these crazy contests. Ms. Shottlan was one of the most creative. She'd thought up the Worm Sundae Slide, where students had to crawl on their bellies across a tarp covered in choco- late sauce, sprinkles, and whipped cream. Everyone went home a sticky, gooey mess—but it was the best day of the entire school year.

Kylie noticed Lexi and Jenna waving at her from the picnic area and she ran over.

"How are we doing?" she asked. Jenna held up a cupcake piped with green "grass" frosting. On the top was a fondant bear—the Blakely mascot.

"Our Beary Special Field Day cupcakes are a huge hit," Jenna said. "It was utter genius, Kylie, to do a green velvet cupcake. Principal Fontina had two of them."

"I think our class is about to have a tug-of-war," Lexi said, pointing in the direction of the soccer field. Ms. Shottlan was lining up her classmates on opposite sides of a long rope.

"Gotta run!" said Kylie. When she got to the rope, she noticed that Ms. Shottlan was pouring something all over it.

"Liquid soap!" her teacher grinned. "Makes it a little tougher to get a grip!"

Kylie took a spot behind Emily on the left side of the rope. Ms. Shottlan did a quick count. "I need one more person on the left to even it out," she said. "Meredith, come on over and grab on behind Kylie."

Kylie gulped. The idea of Meredith looming over her shoulder still scared her—even though her dad had promised there would be no more bullying and Meredith had called and said, "Sorry." Meredith took the rope without a word. That was a good sign, Kylie thought, but then again, she never knew when Meredith might launch a sneak attack.

As Mr. C., the gym teacher, blew his whistle, the kids began pulling with all their might.

"Go! Go! Go!" screamed Jeremy, who was captaining the left team. Kylie tried to hold tight to the rope, but it kept slipping through her fingers. "I'm losing it!" she called.

She could hear Meredith huffing and puffing in her ear. "Oh no! I broke a nail!" she cried.

Abby, on the right, dug her heels into the grass. "Keep...pulling...*hard*!" she coached as her side slowly began to gain ground. With one last big tug, everyone on the left side lost their grip and went sprawling on their backs. They collapsed in a heap, and at the very bottom was Meredith.

"Get off! Get off!" she shrieked. Kylie stumbled to her feet. She looked at Meredith, who was covered in grass stains and dirt, and her perfect curls were matted with mud. Her face was beet red. She looked like a volcano about to erupt.

But instead she let out a high-pitched cry. "Oh noooooooooo!" she wailed. At first Kylie thought she was upset over her ruined manicure. But then Meredith began to scream, "My necklace! My diamond M—it's missing!" She dug frantically through the dirt.

Everyone crawled around on the grass, trying to help her find it.

"When did you last see it?" asked Ms. Shottlan.

"I don't know," whimpered Meredith. "After the water-balloon toss? Or maybe right before lunch?"

After fifteen minutes, there still was no sign of Meredith's M—and she was inconsolable.

"I'm sure your mom will buy you another one," Emily tried to comfort her.

"No. I'm grounded." Meredith glared at Kylie. "No shopping for the rest of the semester."

Kylie walked away. She wanted to gloat, but part of her felt bad for Meredith, who was simply devastated by losing her favorite necklace. Kylie remembered when she was eight and had lost the iPod her parents bought her for her birthday. She knew she had it with her when they went to the park, but when she checked her pockets…gone. She had cried for two days, especially because her mom and dad had said she couldn't have another one because she had been careless. It had taken her a whole year of saving her allowance to afford a replacement.

She glanced back at Meredith sobbing on the soccer field. Her mom would probably be even tougher on her than Kylie's parents had been. Mrs. Mitchell didn't seem like a person you wanted mad at you.

"What happened to Meredith?" asked Sadie.

"She lost her bling," Kylie replied. "You know—her diamond M necklace?"

"Ouch. That thing probably cost a fortune!" said Jenna, whistling through her teeth.

"We looked everywhere. It's just gone," said Kylie.

"So are all the cupcakes," interrupted Juliette, holding up the last empty tray. "I think you girls should clean up now. Great job, Peace, Love, and Cupcakes!"

As Kylie began to stack the empty trays on the table, she felt something hard crunch under her sneaker. She saw a glint of something in the dirt.

"Meredith's necklace!" she said, gingerly picking it out of the grass and dusting it off.

"No way!" said Jenna. "What are you going to do with it?"

Kylie cradled the necklace in her palm. The chain had broken, but the M was just fine.

"What do you think I should do?" she asked her fellow club members.

Sadie bit her lip. "I want to say keep it for a week and make Meredith sweat, but I guess that's not the nicest thing to do, right?"

"Sell it on eBay?" Jenna joked.

Kylie thought about how she'd felt when she lost her iPod—and that didn't even have any sentimental value. She pictured her most precious, prized possession: a pearl ring that her great-grandma Chicky had given to her. Kylie kept it carefully locked away in her jewelry box. It was more than one hundred years old and had belonged to Mama Chicky as a child. Right before she died, she'd told Kylie she wanted her to have it. If she lost that ring, her heart would be broken.

"Meredith!" Kylie shouted from across the field. She ran toward her, her hand extended.

"What do *you* want?" sniffed Meredith when Kylie was standing only inches away.

"I found this—by the picnic table. You must have dropped it at lunch." She handed Meredith her necklace.

"Oh my gosh! My necklace!" Meredith squealed. Then she did something Kylie never saw coming: she grabbed her and hugged her. It was a sneak attack, all right, but not the kind Kylie had envisioned!

She was speechless. She had expected Meredith to accuse her of stealing the necklace—or at the very least, to scold her for taking so long to find it. But instead Meredith just smiled and ran off to show Ms. Shottlan that her pendant had been found.

Kylie's head was spinning. Jenna, Lexi, and Sadie looked equally stunned when she came back to the picnic area.

"Did I just see what I think I saw?" asked Sadie.

Jenna peered over Kylie's shoulder. "Just checking to make sure she didn't put a 'Kick Me' sign on you or something." She giggled. "Nope, you're clear!"

"I think she learned her lesson," said Kylie. "Who knows, maybe Meredith and I are going to be BFFs from now on."

The girls looked at each other then burst out laughing.

"Nah." Kylie laughed as well. "But it doesn't matter—because I have the best friends any cupcake-club president could ever ask for. You guys wanna come over tonight for a sleepover? I have a great DVD—*Annie Get Your*

Gun—and an amazing recipe I want to try for key lime pie cupcakes."

"Cupcakes? Count me in!" said Jenna.

"Sounds fun," said Lexi.

Then Sadie took off three of her Field Day gold medals and placed one around each girl's neck.

"What's this for?" asked Kylie.

"For the coolest cupcake bakers at Blakely," she said.

"In New Fairfield," said Lexi.

"In the entire world!" exclaimed Jenna.

Kylie smiled. Not yet, but someday…soon.

Juliette's Red Velvet Cupcakes with Maple Cream Cheese Frosting

Red Velvet Cupcakes

Makes 18

- ½ cup vegetable shortening
- 1½ cups sugar
- 2 eggs
- 1 teaspoon vanilla
- 1¼ cup buttermilk
- Red food coloring

    (Note: We like gel food coloring, as it creates clearer colors. If using liquid coloring, reduce milk by the same amount so you don't add too much liquid.)

- 2½ cups all-purpose flour
- 2 tablespoons cocoa powder
- 1 teaspoon baking soda
- 1 teaspoon salt

Directions

1. Preheat oven to 350°F.
2. Using an electric mixer, cream shortening and sugar together until light and fluffy.
3. Mix in eggs, one at a time. Add vanilla and buttermilk.
4. Carefully add food coloring until you reach your desired color.
5. In a separate bowl, whisk together flour, cocoa powder, baking soda, and salt.
6. Gradually mix the dry ingredients into the wet ingredients until just combined. Be careful not to over mix.
7. Spoon mixture into cupcake pan prepared with paper liners, filling each cup two-thirds full.
8. Bake for 20–25 minutes. Use a toothpick to test for doneness.
9. Transfer cupcakes to a wire rack to cool.

Maple Cream Cheese Frosting

1 stick butter

1 cup cream cheese

4 cups confectioners' sugar

2 teaspoons vanilla

Pinch of salt

2 tablespoons maple syrup

Brown sugar for topping (optional)

Directions

1. Using an electric mixer, whip butter and cream cheese until light and fluffy.

2. Add 2 cups of confectioners' sugar, starting with the mixer on slow and speeding up until well mixed.

3. Add vanilla, salt, and maple syrup. Mix well.

4. Add remaining confectioners' sugar, 1 cup at a time. Whip on high speed.

5. If frosting is too soft, add more confectioners' sugar ½ cup at a time until desired consistency. If frosting is too thick, add a splash of maple syrup.

6. Generously frost the top of cooled cupcakes and sprinkle with brown sugar to add a delicious crunch.

Eco-licious Chocolate Cupcakes

Chocolate Cupcakes

Makes 18

- 1¼ cups flour
- ¾ teaspoon baking soda
- ½ teaspoon salt
- 1 cup organic cocoa powder
- 1 cup boiling water
- 2 teaspoons vanilla
- ½ cup sour cream
- 2 sticks butter
- 1¾ cups sugar
- 2 eggs

Directions

1. Preheat oven to 350°F.
2. In a medium bowl, measure flour, baking soda, and salt to make the flour mixture. Whisk together, and set aside.
3. In a separate bowl, add boiling water to cocoa powder.

Be very careful not to burn yourself! Whisk until smooth. Add vanilla and sour cream and stir to combine to make the chocolate mixture.

4. In a third bowl, use an electric mixer to cream the butter and sugar together until light and fluffy.

5. Add eggs, one at a time, mixing well after each egg.

6. With the mixer on low, alternate adding a third of the flour mixture and a third of the chocolate mixture. Continue until all is added. Be careful not to over mix.

7. Spoon mixture into cupcake pan prepared with paper liners, filling each cup two-thirds full.

8. Bake for 20–25 minutes. Use a toothpick to test for doneness.

9. Transfer cupcakes to a wire rack to cool.

Organic Chocolate Frosting

9 ounces organic chocolate

2 sticks butter

⅓ cup light corn syrup

Pinch of salt

Chocolate nibs or mini chocolate chips (optional, for decoration)

Mint leaves (optional, for garnish)

Directions

1. In a medium bowl, melt butter and chocolate together in the microwave, and stir until smooth. Heat in 30-second increments, stirring between each, and being careful not to burn the chocolate.

2. When the chocolate is melted, add corn syrup and salt, and stir until well combined.

3. Let sit to cool. Stir occasionally until frosting is thick enough to spread.

4. Dip the top of a cooled cupcake into the frosting and remove while twisting the cupcake to allow any excess to drip off.

5. Before the frosting sets, sprinkle with chocolate nibs or mini chocolate chips and garnish with a mint leaf.

The Sweet Revenge Cannoli Cupcake

Vanilla Cupcakes
Makes 12

- 1 stick butter, at room temperature
- ¾ cup + 2 tablespoons sugar
- 2 large eggs
- 1 teaspoon vanilla
- 1½ cups all-purpose flour
- 1½ teaspoons baking powder
- ¼ teaspoon salt
- ½ cup + 2 tablespoons milk

Directions

1. Preheat oven to 350°F.
2. Using an electric mixer, mix butter and sugar together until light and fluffy.
3. Mix in eggs, one at a time. Add vanilla.
4. In a separate bowl, whisk together flour, baking powder, and salt to make the flour mixture.

5. Alternate adding the flour mixture and milk, adding each in three separate parts and beginning and ending with the flour. Mix until combined after each addition.

6. Spoon mixture into cupcake pan prepared with paper liners, filling each cup two-thirds full.

7. Bake until golden brown. Use a toothpick to test for doneness.

8. Transfer cupcakes to a wire rack to cool.

Ricotta Frosting

1 stick butter, at room temperature

½ cup ricotta cheese

4½ cups confectioners' sugar

1 teaspoon vanilla

Splash of milk

Pinch of salt

Mini chocolate chips (for decoration)

Pinch of cinnamon (for decoration)

Crumbled ice cream cone (for decoration)

Directions

1. Using an electric mixer, whip butter and ricotta cheese until combined.

2. Add 2 cups of confectioners' sugar to the butter mixture, and starting with the mixer on a slow speed and speeding up until well mixed.

3. Add vanilla, milk, and salt, and mix until combined.

4. Add remaining confectioners' sugar, 1 cup at a time. Whip on high speed.

5. If frosting is too soft, add more confectioners' sugar ½ cup at a time until desired consistency. If frosting is too thick, add a splash of milk.

6. Fill cupcake with a scoop of ricotta frosting.

7. Frost cupcakes, and sprinkle with mini chocolate chips and a pinch of cinnamon.

8. Break an ice cream cone and sprinkle on top of cupcake.

Recipes developed by Jessi Walter, CEO and Chief Bud at Taste Buds (www.tastebudscook.com).

Carrie's Ten Tips for Perfect Cupcakes

1. Make sure you have all the ingredients. Read the whole list first and check off everything carefully. Sometimes a recipe may call for whole milk and you only have skim in the fridge. But using skim can make a big difference in the way the cupcake tastes.

2. Fill your cupcake with something fun. I like to put a surprise in the middle of my cupcakes: like frosting in a bright green color or chocolate fudge that oozes out when you take a bite. That way, you never know what you're going to get!

3. Piping tips can be a fun way to get a great look for your frosting. Try out your tip before you use it on a cupcake, though. Sometimes it will make a pattern you don't love. My favorite is a star tip.

4. Use real fresh fruit in your cupcakes. My favorites are banana, strawberries, blueberries, and apple. They can make a plain vanilla cupcake taste yummy. And it's healthier too!

5. Don't pile too much frosting on your cupcake. I don't like a mountain on mine. I think you should be able to taste both the cake and the frosting, not just the frosting.

6. Don't forget to dress up your cupcakes. I love pretty wrappers, toppers, picks, sprinkles, and colored sugar. I also love making things out of fondant—it looks so professional!

7. Let your cupcakes cool before you frost them. If you don't, the icing will melt and roll off the cupcake and you'll have a sticky mess!

8. If you're using a piping bag, fasten the top with a rubber band or a clip. Otherwise the frosting squeezes out the top, and you have to lick it off your hands. (Well, not a bad thing…)

9. Pipe in one smooth circular motion—not little squeezes, which will look uneven. The smoother you go, the more professional your cupcake will look.

10. Share your cupcakes! It's the best way to get feedback on your recipes and learn what you need to do to improve. Give some to your neighbors, your teachers, and your friends, and ask for their critique.

For more tips and cupcake info, go to www.carriescupcake critique.shutterfly.com. You can also email Carrie at carrie plcclub@aol.com

Acknowledgments

We couldn't have written this book without the love and support of the following people:

Peter/Daddy: Thank you for taking us to all those cupcake stores for research and for being the best husband and father in the world! We love you to the moon!

Our family: Gaga Judy Kahn (the world's best playdate!) and Aunt Debbie; Papa and Gram Bobbi; Charles, Peggy, Brad, and all the Saperstones: Nancy, Peter, Emily, Jack, and Jason. Hugs and sprinkles to you all! And Mama Chickie: a great baker and a great lady.

Our brilliant recipe developer, Jessi Walter of Taste Buds. Working with you is so yummy, and we are so grateful to have you be a part of this series!

Our PS 6 Family: Lauren Fontana, Amy Santucci, Daniel Kim, Emily Schottland, Jackie Levenherz, Michelle Fein, Rachel Stander, Rachel Weis, Kim Bader, Rebecca

Satten, and the PS 6 Eric Dutt Eco Center. Thank you all for teaching Carrie to reach for the stars and write from the heart.

Carrie's BFFs, who inspire us (and make us smile!): Darby Dutter, Jaimie Ludwig, Bella Camaj, Abby Johnson, Ava Nobandegani, Sadie and Lila Goldstein, and Juliette Andre.

Sheryl's BFFs, who cheerlead her onward and upward always: Kathy Passero, Holly Russell, Stacy Polsky, and Debbie Skolnik.

The sweet professionals who have been so supportive of Carrie's Cupcake Critique blog: Katherine Kallinis and Sophie LaMontagne of *DC Cupcakes*; *Cake Boss* Buddy Valastro; *Staten Island Cake's* Vinny Buzzetta; Sticky Fingers' Doron Peterson; Crumbs CEO Jason Bauer; Sprinkles founder and *Cupcake Wars* judge Candace Nelson; Rachel Kramer Bussell and Nichelle Stephens of *Cupcakes Take the Cake* blog; and Dylan Lauren of Dylan's Candy Bar.

Our editors at Sourcebooks/Jabberwocky, who have made working on this fiction series such a delectable experience: Leah Hultenschmidt and Rebecca Frazer. And all the support from Aubrey Poole, Kelly Barrales-Saylor, Steve Geck, Kristin Zelazko, and Todd Stocke.

Our agents at The Literary Group: Frank Weimann, Katherine Latshaw, and Elyse Tanzillo.

To read *Carrie's Cupcake Critique* blog, go to www.carries cupcakecritique.shutterfly.com and follow her on Twitter @CBCupcakeCritic.

To make a donation to the PS 6 Eric Dutt Eco Center, send a check payable to PS 6 Alumni Foundation Co. with Eco Center noted on the memo line to:

PS 6 Alumni Foundation Co.

45 East 81st Street

New York, NY 10028

Join the Peace, Love, and Cupcake Club on their next delicious adventure!

Coming Soon!

About the Authors

Photo by Heidi Green

New York Times bestselling author Sheryl Berk was the founding editor in chief of *Life & Style Weekly* as well as a contributor to *InStyle*, *Martha Stewart*, and other publications. She has written dozens of books with celebrities, including Britney Spears, Whitney Port, Bethany Hamilton (*Soul Surfer*), Tia Mowry, and *Jersey Shore*'s JWOWW. Her nine-year-old daughter, Carrie Berk, a cupcake connoisseur and blogger, cooked up the idea for the PLC series in second grade. Together they have invented dozens of crazy cupcake recipes in their New York City kitchen (Can you say "purple velvet"?) and have the frosting stains on the ceiling to prove it. They love writing together and have many more adventures in store for the PLC girls!

WITHDRAWN